Paint
it
Blue

George Thomas Clark

Published by GeorgeThomasClark.com

ISBN: 978-0-9910623-6-2– Trade Paperback (revised)

GeorgeThomasClark.com
Bakersfield, California
webmaster@GeorgeThomasClark.com

Books by George Thomas Clark

Hitler Here
The Bold Investor
Death in the Ring
King Donald
Echoes from Saddam Hussein
Obama on Edge
Tales of Romance
In Other Hands
Paint it Blue

Introduction

We wonder what they're thinking, so we ask Frida Kahlo and Diego Rivera. And you, Picasso, what are you really like? Vincent van Gogh, please tell us more about your agony and inspiration. We must also learn about distinguished women – Paula Modersohn-Becker, Séraphine Louis, Lee Krasner, Diane Arbus, and others. I know they'll tell us. So will expressionists like Ernst Ludwig Kirschner and Otto Dix. African American artists are certainly forthcoming. Charles White takes us inside his homes, and William H. Johnson invites us into his mind, a stimulating but often unsafe place. And other painters from Europe and the United States – what are they feeling? We find out as they *Paint It Blue*.

Contents

Frida and Diego

In the Blue House

It can't be too late. This is a meeting so compelling and mandatory that all rules, technicalities, and encumbrances must be ignored. It doesn't matter they are dead. It doesn't matter they never knew each other. It doesn't matter they were married. It matters only that the proper time be chosen, a common instant that allows both to be decently pubescent and artistically aware. It must as well be long before dissipation and obscene fate ravaged their bodies and eviscerated their souls. The moment, indeed, must be entirely propitious when Papa comes to Frida's house.

It's a blue house, and Frida was born there and she will die there. She will always be there. It's her house and she's searching for another woman who's been sleeping with Diego. The intruder's healthy and hot and new, and Diego's been pounding her with three hundred passionate pounds, and every thrust fractures Frida's bones. But Frida can't find her. The other woman is not in the blue house. She must be somewhere with Diego right now, and Frida can hear everything and wants to kill them both. Maybe more she wants Diego to kill her. She wants him to stab her into oblivion. She certainly wants something. She must absolutely have something, but it might not be revenge or the oblivion of alcohol and drugs, which won't suppress her pain.

No, there must be something else. There must be something better. There must be something to help her forget all this, and it must relieve her right away. She doesn't know what it could be. She can't imagine how to escape. She doesn't know how to get out of the blue prison. But today she does not need to. Today Papa is standing at the door, knocking. The servants are not there. Frida is alone, wearing a Tehuana dress long to the floor. She opens the door and looks at Papa. He is strong and brown and his mustache makes him look like Gable. The poet MacLeish has said oxygen is sucked from a room when Papa enters. He's in the blue house and Frida sighs.

She knows she can have him. She can have almost any man or woman she wants, for awhile. Language is certainly not a problem. Papa speaks Spanish. Frida speaks English. Papa's more Latin than Frida feels Anglo. They talk Spanish, and are funny and flirtatious in the relaxed Latin way. Frida is delighted. So is Papa. This is good for him, too. He is tired of his second wife. He doesn't want her anymore just as he had not wanted his first wife anymore. He has also gotten tired of his first blonde girlfriend, a Grace Kelly twenty years before the real one. Actually, Papa is not so much tired of the blonde. He is tired she's so beautiful and rich he can't have her. He can have her sometimes, but he can't really have her. He doesn't need her. Frida is standing before him in her Tehuana dress.

Papa understands painters. He knows Picasso and Miró, and he knows about Diego. But he doesn't know Frida. She shows him her work, the self-portraits of a queen, a queen covered with tears and blood and scars, surrounded by fetuses and bones and death, and she has an eye in her forehead, and in the eye there is Diego, and Diego will always be at the center of her, but right now, today, Papa is there, and there are no tears in Frida's eyes.

She is looking at Papa. She has read his short stories in English and senses he is the best young American writer ever. He is a gringo writer but his canvas is the world. He knows what he is but can't imagine that is more than he ever again will be. Frida, even after studying her masterpieces, is not sure what she is. Papa tells her. He tells her: "Frida, you are."

Then he kisses her. He is thankful he's had some practice with the blonde, his first beautiful woman. That makes this easier and better. He doesn't have to worry Frida is too good for him. He feels great embracing her. She sticks her tongue in his mouth, and he pushes himself hard against her Tehuana dress and sucks on her hot face and neck. She's sighing and pulling at the shirt on his big shoulders. He picks her up and asks where. She points, and he carries her into the bedroom and sets her on her feet, reaching for the back of her Tehuana dress.

"Espera," she says. "My right leg. You should know. I had polio. And the trolley. It hit the bus I was on. I'm not what you think."

He doesn't care. Trotsky won't either. No sane man would. Frida is taking off her Tehuana dress. Papa grabs his belt and she helps him and they embrace again then fall onto the bed and soon Frida's aroused and saying sweet things and Papa's sweaty and she's shouting now and he loves that and at the end exclaims: "Frida."

"Gracias," she says.

This is what Papa needs, too. It's difficult trying to be not only what he is, but what he says he is. He often says he's brave and tough and graceful, in addition to the real stuff, and all that is hard to maintain. Papa's father shot himself a decade earlier, and his brother is also going to kill himself and so are a sister and granddaughter, and one of his sons will crave to be a woman. Papa often talks about suicide and knows he'll someday have to shoot himself unless someone shoots him first. That's why he loves war. He doesn't want to be a real soldier and have to be there all the time. He wants to go there when he needs it, and be shot at when he wants it. Papa doesn't realize Frida knows more about her death than he does his. During the Great War only his wounded leg was at stake. In a smashed bus when she was eighteen, the naked and bloody Frida was considered good as dead.

"Listen," she says.

"What?"

"At the front door."

"Who?"

"Diego. You've got to get out or he'll kill you."

Papa lumbers up and puts on his pants.

"Apúrate. Diego always carries a gun."

Papa doesn't have any of his guns so crouches next to the wall on the side the door could swing.

Big footsteps come down the hall.

"Go out the window."

"Too late."

"Frida, are you in there?"

"Sí, Diego. Un minutico."

The door flies open and Diego, grinning in a huge face, storms in to see his wife sitting on the bed, holding a sheet with both hands against her neck.

"Frida," he shouts, and instinctively wheels around.

Now, the fat man, who as a fat youth fought anyone who challenged him, stands looking at a bare-chested man in his bedroom. Then he charges Papa. Rather than sidestepping and attacking obliquely, as one would a bull, Papa steps fast forward and nails Diego with a right cross to the jaw. Diego staggers but keeps lumbering and grabs him by the throat. Papa thrusts his hands underneath to Diego's neck but can't get a good grip. Diego has a very strong grip, and forces Papa back against the wall. He feels his neck burn. Diego snarls and squeezes harder until Papa fires a left hook over Diego's arms and nails his right jaw, breaking the grip. Then Papa throws a right and a left to the huge stomach of Diego, who gasps but continues to grapple, and both men roll to the floor. Papa is quicker and bounds over on top and shoves his right palm into Diego's face and begins firing short left hooks, landing most until he shrieks.

"Out," Frida demands, standing nude above them, holding a palette knife.

George Thomas Clark

Frida Celebrates Centennial

Thousands of people every day line up outside Mexico City's eminent cultural center – Palacio de Bellas Artes – then with reverence and enthusiasm enter the primary gallery where sixty-five oil paintings, declarations of my life, are displayed to celebrate not merely my aesthetic vision but my glamorous and wretched journey, and, I shudder, my one-hundredth birthday. I know you're examining my pictures the same way I looked into the mirror before painting self-portraits, and have always considered me young. No one who dies at age forty-seven will ever be old.

If healthy I would have happily forsaken everlasting youth and endured a century to see my work in a comprehensive exhibition in Mexico. During my lifetime, and then only a year before the end when they carried me in on my bed, I had but a single one-woman show at a gallery. Most didn't consider that a slight. I was a woman in a world of machismo, and my man, Diego Rivera, was the greatest painter in it. I've had to keep working after death, as all great artists should, to build my reputation and celebrity and become the first Latin artist, male or female, whose single work commanded more than a million dollars. My record prices keep soaring, and even more stunningly I continue to grow as cultural hero and marketing cliché, as a beautiful woman and disfigured invalid, as a powerful spirit with shattered soul.

Henceforth, that is going to change. At least some of it will. Together we will discover the new Frida, not the one who as an eighteen-year old suffered multiple fractures of my spinal column and pelvis and right leg and several other bones, and was impaled by a metal pole from hip through abdomen, and shrieked louder than approaching sirens when a man at the scene put his foot on my body and pulled out the spear. No, I'm not getting on that flimsy wooden bus in September 1925. I won't be around when the trolley car strikes. I'm not going through that, though I'm sure most of you believe I wouldn't have become a legendary artist without overwhelming pain. I did need suffering, but not so much.

Let's move into the main gallery and join the masses moving slowly in front of my paintings on walls in the high-ceiling room. There, look at that self-portrait from 1926, only a year after the accident. I'm not showing any trauma, just (for the first time) beautiful strokes of portraiture one simply doesn't forget. But that one, *Henry Ford Hospital*, with me hemorrhaging on a bed surrounded by a pelvis, fetus and dead child, could not have been painted without the crash. Nor could I have portrayed myself grimly sitting on a bed next to another lifeless baby, a horrid creature, in *Me and My Doll*.

Now, with vigor, I won't have three miscarriages, and Diego and I will welcome a child or two – whether or not he wants them – and I'll depict myself as a mother and, perhaps less self-obsessively, portray the children growing up in the home of a three-hundred-pound workaholic genius and communist child who rarely bathes and constantly chases and is chased by women. There, look at *Frida and Diego Rivera*. What a happy couple we seem to be. In fact we were quite happy then in San Francisco. Diego was painting murals and I painted us holding hands and will do that again in *Self-Portrait on the Border between Mexico and the Untied States*. I'm a pink-dress-wearing, flag-holding-Mexican patriot living in industrial-smoke-spitting America but yearning for the temples and fertility of my native land. I'll certainly also paint *Self-Portrait with Necklace*, though the jewelry might this time look a little less like a choke chain.

Some paintings simply didn't require more than thirty operations and thousands of narcotic injections and an eternity in casts and corsets alone in bed. I'm confident I'll still do my celebrated self-portraits with my monkeys and parrots. These are depictions of elegance and nature, not of a ruptured psyche. But I did need suffering to paint my exposed hearts in *The Two Fridas* and brush a skull between my eyes while *Thinking about Death*. And I projected pain onto canvas in *The Broken Column*, open and shattered from neck to pelvis while my flesh is wounded by nails and tears crawl down my cheeks.

Inevitably, much of my work will be different, but I can draw on some of the same problems. I was obsessive about my first boyfriend, even before the crash, so I can in many ways continue to paint my fixation on Diego. But henceforth my images will be stronger and more aggressive. Rather than weep or bleed when he betrays me, I'll pummel him. And instead of occasionally making love to other men and women, I'll do so with scores and follow with portrayals to show Diego and everyone else.

I'll unavoidably retain my depressive nature. As a teenager I wrote letters about suffering and pain and sadness, and being obliged to bear them, and all that I can use in my work. I'll also concentrate more on my alcoholism. *The Two (New) Fridas,* hearts unseen, will be holding hands side by side on the bed, and one will be rumpled, weeping, and drunk, and the other stylish, stoic, and sober. I don't need to paint damaged bones and bleeding flesh to be a seminal artist. I still have my astonishing face and magnetism, and the same imagination and precise brushstrokes to convey what I feel. I'll be an even better Frida you again celebrate at Bellas Artes

Diego Denies his Art Naïve

I'm weary of being hounded about my political beliefs, which I'm prouder of than anything except my murals and paintings. People still say, "How could so gifted an artist be such a political nincompoop?" Perhaps, then, I should respond that though I was an ardent communist until my death a half century ago, I wouldn't be a communist today. I'd probably be a compassionate socialist. I certainly wouldn't be a Stalinist. I hope I wouldn't. But maybe I would. Let's take a look and decide.

From Mexico in the early 1930's I was beckoned into the heart of capitalism and for the Fords in Detroit painted a mural called *Man and Machine* celebrating the might of industrial America. The Rockefellers then summoned me to New York to create *Man at the Crossroads* for the RCA building still under construction. All of my preliminary drawings were approved and Abby, mother of Nelson and John D. Rockefeller., bought my sketchbook. Of course, as an artist, I made a few late-stage creative changes, and the image of Lenin appears joining hands with the people, uniting them in communist brotherhood. The Rockefeller brothers ordered me to paint over Lenin's face. I refused. They sent the police in, removed me from the premises, paid me off, covered the mural, and finally destroyed it the following year, 1934.

I responded by recreating a slightly smaller version, newly titled *Man, Controller of the Universe,* at Palacio de Bellas Artes in Mexico City. A huge blond man is at the center of the work, controlling the levers at the center of human existence, at the crossroads, that is. On the viewers' left side I offer capitalism, a corrupt and horrific system symbolized by a man wearing a heavy cross around his neck above arms with no hands. In the top left, helmeted and gas-masked troops carry rifles with bayonets slanted at a cloudy, warplane-filled sky. They are protectors of an exploitative system that requires, in my mural images, horse-riding police to club strikers, one holding a sign that says: "We want work, not charity." Gaudy gowned women gamble playing cards while their husbands and other women slurp cocktails and dance in the background. Into this rapacious world I place Darwin over a naked blond baby who's holding a monkey's hand while an ugly dog licks the baby's head which looks down on a

9

turtle.

On the righteous side I present the human-hand-holding Lenin surrounded by workers who adore him. Further right, or to the far left of those in the painting, a friendly, professorial Trotsky stands at the center of delighted and determined workers. And in the top corner, I show ever more aroused workers, ready for capitalist forces on the opposite side. A massive machine separates them. The communist workers are backed by an army armed only with red flags. Into this harmony I paint pretty female athletes, clad in white shirts and shorts, poised and ready to charge into the universal future.

Today, I would not claim these images and symbols accurately reflect what has happened in the world since 1934. A far more prescient painting is right around the corner in Belles Artes. It is a small work in a hall of vast murals. And I should concede that in this palace the works of the other two Tres Grandes of Mexico – Jose Clemente Orozco and David Alfaro Siqueiros – at times overwhelm my didactic efforts. Rather than preach, their murals roar. And reasonable viewers understand their status and fame would be greater if only they'd had my charisma as well as an elegant, photogenic, obsessive, crippled, alcoholic, drug-addicted, bisexual, cult-inspiring, great-painting wife like Frida Kahlo. I'm not bowing to Orozco and Siqueiros, merely acknowledging they're equals.

And that small 1933 painting of such foresight, it's called *Russian Revolution or Third International.* Lenin and Trotsky stand monumentally as guides of the Red Army. In front of the two great leaders people of different nationalities represent the international proletariat gathering to hear the distinguished Soviet messengers. They are backed on one side by a massive group of red-star and helmet-with-face-guard soldiers and on the other by workers with firearms. It is a dark and troubling scene and foretells millions of murders to be committed by the Soviet leaders, especially Stalin. But wait. I have pointedly omitted Stalin. I'd already met the swine and considered him artistically limited and quite restrictive. And don't blame me about Lenin. He'd been dead since 1924. Don't impugn Trotsky, either. He was in exile, forever running from Stalin's assassins.

In 1937 Frida and I welcomed him into our Blue House and provided four safe walls. Trotsky responded by frequently quarreling with me and sleeping with Frida as often as he could. Frida was still striking back at me for having an affair with her sister Cristina a few years earlier. I don't think she liked the old man much. He at any rate moved out after two years and lived nearby under strong protection that nevertheless failed to prevent an axe being buried in his head. Authorities questioned Frida for twelve hours and tried to blame me too. I was out of the country. Eventually, we were cleared.

I wouldn't have hurt my communist brother Trotsky. We had so much in common. Like most influential communists, we loved luxury. I owned the spacious Blue House built along walls surrounding trees and a garden. I'd bought it from Frida's father to help him out of debt. I also owned two stylish and elevated studios, one each for Frida and me. They were connected by a bridge. Huge windows allowed me to peer into trees that shaded my studio just right. Many important people came to visit and be painted. Glamorous actresses Paulette Goddard and Dolores del Rio and Maria Felix are just three who posed and more. I also knew presidents and industrialists and revolutionaries and writers. I really didn't know too many workers but was certainly earthy and charming whenever I passed among them. I just didn't live like them. I was an elite communist. And elite communists live like capitalists. I think I realized that. People tried to help me understand. The communists who expelled me from the party in Mexico accused me of being a "painter of palaces for Yankee tourists." My enemies would've painted or lived in palaces if they could. That's the nature of man. It just wasn't a theme of my murals.

Critics should remember that in a 1940 article for *Esquire* magazine I called Stalin the "undertaker of the Russian revolution." I knew what he'd done to the peasantry of the Soviet Union during the 1930's. I put that aside in June 1941 when the Nazis attacked the communists. My brothers and sisters were fighting to avoid national extermination. Fearless leader Stalin absorbed the Wehrmacht's devastating strikes and rallied the people to survive, to resist, to counterattack and destroy fascism. That is Stalin's greatest contribution. I celebrated it in my 1952 Mural *The Nightmare of War and the Dream of Peace.* A gleaming, fatherly Stalin, accompanied by handsome young Mao, offers a white dove to sinister capitalist leaders who stand in front of, and apart from, their nightmarish world of fighting and lynching and a black man nailed to a cross. Capitalists need to realize the two communist titans are not mass murderers but men of peace. Embrace these communist brothers. Be like them. Better, be like me. Live far away from Stalin and Mao, and flourish in a world of luxury and hypocrisy and extraordinary art.

Ramos Martinez Debates Rivera

"You'll never be in the first rank of Mexican artists because your work lacks political dimension," said Diego Rivera.

"Let me refute that, for your edification, of course," said Manuel Ramos Martínez. "Please, step inside for my exhibition at the Pasadena Museum of California Art."

"Quite a modest place next to the grand museums that host my work."

"Celebrity, I must grant you. But I believe much of your antipathy – is it jealously, too? – derives from the conviction of Ramón Alva de la Canal, shared by many other Mexican artists, that 'the true force behind contemporary Mexican painting isn't Diego Rivera; it is Alfredo Ramos Martínez.'

"Let's begin here. Is this painting not inherently political, a proud but defeated indigenous man bound by ropes around neck and torso in *The Bondage of War*? And this *Man in Bondage* is similarly restricted."

Rivera studied the paintings, right hand supporting his massive double chin and left hand bracing his right elbow.

"In fact, Diego, even my scenes of daily life imply political repression. Behold this *Indian Couple* exhausted by a system that forever either belittles or ignores them. They have no education, no prospects. We were born much lighter and more affluent so don't really understand their world. We only paint it. Thankfully, I'm not this poor man strapped to a basket he struggles to support while *Returning Home from the Market*. And over there my *Indian Mother*, her breasts worn and drooping, struggles to stay awake as she holds her sleeping baby.

"These, Diego, are not the sugary portraits of rich people you paint for fat commissions. Not that I turn down such work, either. I trust you'll appreciate *Calla Lily Vendor*, a dark native woman who's alive and beautiful and aroused by sensuous flowers she holds in a basket on her back."

"A delightful model," says Rivera. "I must paint her. I hope you'll direct me."

"Given your proclivities, I'm afraid not."

"That's the issue, I now understand. It's not your art I dislike, it's you."

Diego Tours Rivera Museum

Don't call it my house. It never was. My father taught school and couldn't buy the place. We only rented the first floor where my twin brother died when we were one. I don't much remember the house or the primitive town of Guanajuato and don't want to. I only recall the bourgeoisie hated my father because he told students that wealthy citizens daily violated indigenous Mexicans and the poor. Señor Rivera, you better leave while you can, they warned. Fine, my father said, I'll live among cultured people in Mexico City, where we moved in 1892. I was six and, until today, returned but once to Guanajuato, in 1956, to see the exterior of the house. My final wife and two daughters from an earlier union and my entourage posed for pictures outside and within hours left the backwater. Why are you taking me there now?

All right, I concede the town has grown most impressively and the surrounding hills host a rainbow of houses, a delightful pallet. Teatro Juarez is certainly a grand structure and there are many others. Fine, let's walk to my family home owned by landlords. The lady wants me to pay. Madame, please look at me carefully. Thank you, I too am honored to be here, and with so many others. Let's see what we have. I doubt those were our chairs, tables, sofa, dreary paintings, or canopied bed next to a crib like the one in which I presumably lay. They seem representative but not that horrid likeness of Frida and me in the corner. Is it papier-mâché? Doesn't matter. I assume they have better art.

All right, show me. What a marvelous contemporary exhibit. These young people can paint. They'll be in museums someday. Indeed, they're already in Casa Museo Diego Rivera. It's recently been expanded and offers some of my works on the second floor? Of course I can walk but we'll take that silver elevator. There's *La Era* I painted in 1904 at age eighteen, a traditional landscape of mountains fronted by two horses, a plow, and a young man in sombrero, waiting to work, finishing work. I let viewers figure it out. I think they'll like *The Forge* from Europe in 1908. I was still quite young and developing as I created this vivid scene of a strong man facing fire from a furnace in an open-front structure covered high by a roof. It may be a bit too realistic by my mature standards but I'm

15

encouraged. Here, from 1910, I recall that young *Breton Girl,* a simple person who suggests buck teeth and tempts me not at all, unlike so many of my later models including actresses and society ladies. No, I'm not boasting. That's part of the historical context. So is the *Marine Rifleman* of 1914. It's distorted. It's strange. It's cubism. I didn't do it long but had to do some because Picasso did and even then I considered him "master of masters."

Really, I didn't find my style until I rediscovered Mexico in 1921. I was thirty-five and had studied and painted fourteen years in Europe and upon returning embraced the indigenous people, seized the powerful, and wrung all their energy and colors onto huge walls of great murals in Mexico City, Chapingo, San Francisco, New York, Detroit. I painted great walls to express the history of Mexico, and when I think of my images, when I see *Bather of Tehuantepec,* here as she was there, a lovely native woman bent at the waist, washing lovely long black Indian hair as brown breasts hang, they hang with soft nipples hard, they hang yearning for love. This is my style. This is my art.

Certainly I had to make a living when I didn't have a mural commission. I bore many expenses, all of Frida's, too, her clothes and jewelry and three dozen surgeries, her house I also bought, yes, La Casa Azul was financially mine though spiritually forever an extension of Frida. That's why I produced handsome but otherwise undistinguished paintings of wealthy people like *Portrait of Alfredo Gomez de la Vega* and the son of Marte Roldolfo Gómez, who was Governor of Tamaulipas. His child I quite well remember. As you see, he was wearing red and unhappily seated to pose for me. Even my jokes didn't much interest him but his big Indian European eyes fascinated me. And now he delights me with news that as a man he donated every painting of mine in the Museo Casa Diego Rivera.

This wonderful space offers even more superb contemporary art on the third floor. We better take the elevator. I see one of my best, *Post-War.* Technically, the war isn't over, it's only 1942, but I knew what had come and would continue, and in response painted this barren tree, almost dead after the fighting, all its branches destroyed, like maimed arms with missing hands, its leaves incinerated, but there is hope in the little green sprout from the slender new branch of a desolate tree.

Paint it Blue

Mexico

George Thomas Clark

Siqueiros Rides Again

Late on a 1940 spring night David Alfaro Siqueiros mounted a horse and ordered comrades from the Spanish Civil War, whom he'd commanded as a tough colonel, and fellow Mexican communists to also mount up and secure their automatic rifles before riding hard to the villa, in Coyoacán south of Mexico City, where Leon Trotsky lived in uneasy exile. That could not continue. Trotsky must die, Siqueiros had determined, because he was against Stalin, the great leader who would create peace and justice and prosperity for all. Siqueiros and his men converged and overpowered the guard in front and then stormed inside, bypassing bribed guards, and fired into Trotsky's bedroom, aiming low, high, and in between, and sustained the barrage until riding away confident they'd killed the eloquent enemy who in fact had hit the floor, crawled behind a heavy bed with his wife, and avoided every bullet.

After hiding in the countryside of Jalisco, Siqueiros was captured. He had already been imprisoned for political activism and would be again. At his trial he displayed theatrical skill, claiming he didn't try to kill Trotsky; he merely sought to provoke an incident that would force the Mexican government to expel the Russian. Siqueiros was acquitted of attempted murder and exiled to Chile instead of being tried on the lesser charges. Shortly, however, the Mexican government summoned him home to paint on a large wall in the elegant Palacio de Belles Artes. In 1944 Stalin was still fighting Hitler, and Siqueiros called his work *The New Democracy*, which, no matter what the artist intended, is not homage to communism but a call for liberty. On a dark and nihilistic battlefield, with a dead soldier naked save for his helmet, there is brightness and hope not asked for but demanded by a beautiful woman with perfect breasts alight and pointed straight at you as she extends strong arms and hands despite her wrists being chained. This is the new democracy of the formerly weak now strengthened by a powerful male left arm, sinews alive in the forearm, thrusting a hard fist to the left of lady liberty.

Soon Siqueiros was back in prison. For his work, that was not always problematic. In 1945 he painted *The Tough Colonel*, he painted himself, that is, as a huge and intrepid warrior brandishing a long arm and fist as formidable as those in the preceding mural. Out of prison

Siqueiros took off everything but his underwear and had his hands tied in front and told the photographer to start shooting. In the photos we see a well-built man a year short of fifty, and in the painting – *Our Present Image*, 1947 – we see much more: two huge, bound hands formed as one, palms up, are extended to say: free my hands and give me my face and individuality rather than this rough rock of a head I hate carrying and you despair looking at.

In 1957 Siqueiros was atop a large hill, the most compelling spot in Mexico City, in Chapultepec Castle, the former home of Maximilian, an Austrian archduke who inbred European noblemen proclaimed Emperor of Mexico in 1864 and three years later was executed for presuming to be so. Siqueiros would have enjoyed being in the firing squad. Now his ammunition was paint he fired to create *From the Dictatorship of Porfirio Diaz to the Revolution*. In one section, Diaz is surrounded by gaudily dressed whores and bourgeois benefactors in top hats. In another, viewers tremble in front of a massive and determined people's army whose soldiers are armed with bayoneted rifles and outfitted with ammunition belts around their torsos. Siqueiros' political candor away from work resulted in accusations, some false, that led to a few more years of age-accelerating imprisonment ending in 1964 when he was sixty-eight. He finished his *Dictatorship* tour de force the following year.

Now David Alfaro Siqueiros is in Los Angeles for exhibitions at the Autry National Museum and the Museum of Latin American Art in Long Beach. He's an artistic hero here, and his work is applauded, studied, preserved, and renovated. In 1932, when he lived in Los Angeles seven months, the response to his work, highlighted by three murals, was paranoid and violent. Since early adulthood Siqueiros had created images that disturbed the bourgeoisie. At the Autry, in *Siqueiros in Los Angeles: Censorship Defied*, his 1930 painting *Penitentiary* shows a faceless poor woman holding a child as they wait, forever, to visit her unseen husband behind bars. In 1931 the person portrayed in *The Yell* howls: it doesn't matter if I'm man or woman or why I'm wearing a cloth on my head, what matters is I'm yelling at you. Siqueiros, under house arrest in Taxco, south of Mexico City, following his first imprisonment, was alerted he might not survive to paint again and escaped to Los Angeles, accompanied by his beautiful girlfriend, the Uruguayan poet Blanca Luz Brum.

George Thomas Clark

On the wall of an Olvera Street building, in the cradle of downtown Los Angeles, Siqueiros painted *Tropical America,* a mural powered by the disturbing image of an indigenous man who, Christ-like, is strangled by rope on a cross that also imprisons his spread hands and feet. Above the corpse is the American eagle. The mural was attacked verbally and then physically and soon whitewashed and, its conquerors assumed, forever covered. But now a restoration team from the Getty Museum is working to retrieve the image that, years after its burial, began to bleed through the whitewash. His mural *Street Scene,* at Chouinard Art Institute where he briefly taught, features a passionate and muscular union man preaching about workers' rights to a racially diverse group, dominated by blacks, who lean to listen from an overhang and more still who listen higher up on the roof. This mural was also whitewashed. Siqueiros prudently painted *Portrait of Mexico Today* in the home of a filmmaker, and it is his only mural in the United States to survive intact and currently resides in the Santa Barbara Museum of Art.

The exhibition at the Museum of Latin American Art is called *Siqueiros: Landscape Painter,* a title that would have amused the artist who forever obsessed about people and politics and used land primarily to convey his convictions. In *Rocky Landscape with Figures* three women, the first with a baby in her arms, walk on cold unforgiving rocks as malicious white clouds gather to strike people and rocks. Nature is no more encouraging in *Urbanization in the Highlands,* a Masada-like plateau crammed with a city imperiled below by a dreary brown world and overhead by angry black clouds. The scene is equally malevolent in *March of Humanity in Latin America* which reveals ant-like people climbing a towering cylindrical landscape to nowhere.

In 1945 Comrade Siqueiros proudly painted *Nationalization of the Oil Industry* to celebrate Mother Earth cradling Mexico's precious oil wells in protective arms that reject Yankee imperialism. Tragically, the goddess could not prevent corrupt Mexican politicians and petro-traffickers from squandering the natural wealth of the nation. Twenty-two years later, in *Oil in Mexico,* he suggests the British Petroleum disaster on a drilling platform rendered helpless in a stormy sea clutched by ominous black sky.

This is the world of Siqueiros, a place of danger and treachery that needs always to be examined and then interpreted in paintings and murals available for everyone to see. His most hopeful work may be *Defense of the Future Victory of Medical Science over Cancer* at the National Medical Center in Mexico City in 1958. A lovely naked female cancer victim, backed by a vast medical team and congregation of loved ones, is about to be pushed into and, presumably, cured by a miraculous radiation machine. It is said that Siqueiros' wife, Angelica Arenal, covered his eyes one day in 1974, as he was dying of cancer, so he could not see his tribute to survival. "Me falta tiempo," he responded.

George Thomas Clark

Hand of Orozco

Chemistry class like all others is boring but mandatory and we're only trying to enliven it with a gunpowder experiment whose eruption prompts a zealous doctor to amputate my left hand and then place his saw on my right before a more stable soul grabs his arm and insists he work to save the hand and forget plucking my injured eye which with thick glasses will help me see and paint a world of indigenous people chained by necks beneath sword-swinging captors who guard financial and religious bloodsuckers.

Campesinos arm and counterattack but their journey is not the ideological fantasy of insulated Rivera but rape and torture and killing. That doesn't change in the forties as swastika strikes hammer and sickle and both hit you before turning on themselves, and in my sixties, tired of insanity and big murals, I paint myself on canvas. As the emerging portrait displeases I shove the handle of a big paint brush into my left eye and another into my upper right cheek and another in my mouth and in my neck and two in my shoulder and pray that will suffice.

Trees of Francisco Goitia

on horses
friend
and i
approach
desert trees
before
we hang
as buzzards
glide

George Thomas Clark

Who is Abraham Angel?

"Where is the National Museum of Art?" I asked numerous people in downtown Mexico City.

"I don't know," they said.

"According to this map, it's got to be near here."

They put palms up.

Indignantly, I wondered how anyone could be unaware of a national treasure so close, and strode around the area, feeling culturally attuned while ignoring the uncomfortable fact that until I opened my eyes in my forties I couldn't have directed anyone to an art museum.

"It's just right down there," a lady ultimately told me.

I'd hit every street in the area but the right one – Tacuba. It's a busy one-way artery three lanes wide, and the National Museum of Art stands as an enormous (yet frequently unseen) neoclassical structure guarded in front by a statue. When it was completed in 1911 and used for government offices, Porfirio Díaz entertained other despots in his ornate second-floor salon. Since 1982 the building has hosted works by Mexico's most gifted painters, particularly from the first half of the twentieth century.

Amid numerous noteworthy offerings – a self-portrait of Jose Clemente Orozco maimed by several paint brushes entering and exiting eyes ears and other parts of his head, and Diego Rivera's image of a stylishly-dressed man holding a glove with a finger serving as the pivot of a Ferris wheel, and the volcanic mountains of Dr. Atl – I noticed a striking male tennis player dressed in navy blue pants and tank top, and surrounded by a pink, purple, light blue, dark green and almost black world at once delightful and ominous. Abraham Angel, the label said, *Portrait of Hugo Tighman.* Next I viewed *Portrait of Esperanza Crespo,* an attractive dark-haired lady of high station who's wearing a dusky blouse and sitting in front of gloomy trees that punch threatening skies. There is another work by Angel. All were made in 1924, his final year of life. Astonishingly, he was born in 1905. So here's a kid who decades ago died at age nineteen and now has three paintings on display in a great museum. Damned impressive, I thought. I wonder what happened to him.

I probably would have left the question there but later in my

Mexico City vacation went to the other side of town, in Chapultepec Park, and entered the Museum of Modern Art where I was overpowered by two massive hands, cupped and supplicating, in front of a faceless face painted by David Alfaro Siqueiros, and enjoyed many other masterworks of Mexican art. Three of those paintings were by Abraham Angel, created in 1923 when he was only eighteen. *The Maid,* pretty and dignified, and *The Little Mule,* stepping through a fantasy village, are bright and vibrant works enlivened by a soothing and deceptively simple style that make Angel's work distinctive. Next to his paintings hangs *Portrait (posthumous) of Abraham Angel,* completed in 1929 by Manuel Rodriguez Lozano. This penetrating work shows a mischievous, slightly aggrieved, and rather effeminate Angel looking askance at a world he has the talent to control. But something happened.

I asked about the tragic young artist but security employees, who'd been following to ensure I didn't touch the paintings, knew nothing about Angel, the labels next to his works having been unseen phenomena. That's all right. They're working low-wage jobs they hope to soon leave. Back home in California, next to my laser printer, I checked the internet and discovered that Abraham Angel, son of a Mexican mother and a father of Scottish ancestry, and youngest of five brothers, had left home at age seventeen, evidently to escape the control of his mother and oldest brother.

He would study art his way. His most influential teacher, not coincidentally, was Manuel Rodriguez Lozano, one of Mexico's finest artists. In addition to painting Angel's portrait, Rodriguez Lozano had been his friend, promoter, and boyfriend. The maestro's emerging homosexuality doubtless disturbed his wife, and the couple divorced.

Abraham Angel and his teacher spent July and August of 1923 together in Cuernavaca, and, as the paintings at the Museum of Modern Art illustrate, this was a period of profound growth and productivity for Angel. Diego Rivera, one of history's most distinguished painters, praised the young man in a contemporary magazine article. According to another web article, Angel in 1924 traveled around Argentina with Rodriguez Lozano and painter Julio Castellanos, exhibiting work to delighted audiences.

Then the road ends. Without explanation or analysis, evidently because of insufficient information, articles declare that in October 1924, at age nineteen, Abraham Angel either committed suicide or died of a cocaine overdose and was buried in a tomb that no longer exists. One is forced to presume that if he did commit suicide, he used cocaine as the fatal weapon. Beyond that, I could only note the colors and psychology of his works had darkened during his final year. I wanted more but even forays through the mammoth marketplace of Amazon.com offered nothing specifically about Angel, and on smaller websites I located two books described as scarce and currently unavailable. Whatever personal information they offer is certain to be a sad and irritatingly incomplete portrait of a young man who, had he survived, would be a giant of modern art. He is not far from that now.

La India of Abraham Angel

i like her
fingers
and hands
on her
long
orange dress
and
her toes
underneath
and especially
i like
her pretty
brown face
and black
hair between
mountains
overlooking
home where
every night
she takes
off her
dress

Forever Alive

They're marching, these dark Mexican men, they're marching and holding sticks in strong hands leading to signs not visible in *La Marcha*, so I ask, "Gentleman, what say you?"

"Ever the same," one answers. "Follow us."

"Where?"

"To another work by Jose Chavez Morado here in Museo del Pueblo."

They lead me to a mural, three sides of a rectangle, and on the left I see a jubilant Spanish conquistador looking to the heavens while forlorn natives starve and try to recover as they wait, for something they wait, probably to die. In the center a man in pointed white hat is manacled around his neck as he also waits. Nearby a nun prays while a European wields the sky to whip a broken-back Indian hauling silver from mines so a wealthy couple can serenely hand money to a beggar, an indigenous boy he is. And who's nearby? A fat-faced king soon to be attacked by an armored warrior on a horse ignited by the fire of four Indians. Next, on the right, a massive American flag envelops that of Mexico while the clergy cringes and gray-old-man government sleeps. He'll wake to a family of conquistadores and Indians holding their ghostly white baby.

"Alarming," I say. "Where next do you go?"

"To Alhóndiga de Granaditas, the public granary where Miguel Hidalgo and other revolutionaries besieged what had become a fortress hiding wealthy Spaniards who lost their wealth when angry people burned down the huge wooden door and besieged the place, killing and burying the Spaniards. Alas, Hidalgo and three other leaders lost their heads which for a decade hung in the corners of Alhóndiga de Granaditas as a warning until independence came."

"I think I understand the general story," I say, standing inside thick walls before a mural and noting manacled slaves and an indigenous mother mourning the child in her arms as a Christian man, bearing a red cross on chest, prepares to plunge a knife into her head. To freedom a skeleton points and an orange-robed savior, sword in sky, breaks his chains and lights a fire of action at the feet of a slumbering indigenous warrior. In the next scene the oppressed attack with spears, clubs, hoes, axes, and sticks, with everything they strike to say you're killing more of us but what you've won is a world of rotting bones.

"Let's go to the home of Jose Chavez Morado," says the man from La Marcha, holding a stick bearing an unseen sign.

"Is he there?"

"Yes, forever."

We march out of downtown Guanajuato into surrounding hills and to a beautiful rock-walled place engulfed by trees and announced by an aqueduct from the seventeenth century.

"Chavez and his wife, artist Olga Costa, born in Germany but a Mexican after age twelve, moved here and began building in the sixties," says the man. "Look at those small bricks in the curved ceiling of their magnificent living room, a room full of religious artifacts though both were atheists."

"Wealthy and atheists – does that bother you?"

"No, because they denounced those who had no conscience and were our people despite Chavez being not merely a celebrated painter but for a long time director of Museo del Pueblo and then Alhóndiga de Granaditas. In daily life I suppose he didn't have so much in common with us but he empathized. Look at Los Galeotes y el Simbolo. Those are galley slaves who were chained below but now stand on deck."

"They're still in chains," I say

"At least they're outside."

"Are Jose and Olga at home?"

"Yes, let's go say hello."

We walk back to a large patio and garden, green and peaceful and bordered by a stone wall.

"Here they are," he says. "In this pot of the siempreviva plant grow the ashes of Olga Costa, 1913-1993, and in that one live the ashes of Jose Chavez Morado, 1909-2002."

George Thomas Clark

Fernando Motilla Emerges

In the hotel dining room I downed fresh fruit and yogurt and warm milk considered cold here. Now, where was the check? I didn't want to wait. It was my first full day in Morelia, the capital of Michoacán about two hundred miles west of Mexico City. I'd done some homework and wanted to get out and see this lovely colonial city's cathedrals and art and the oldest university in all the Americas and the homes and workplaces of revolutionaries and the giant market under an endless tent and narrow stone streets and the aqueduct and much more. Unable to wait I got up and stepped empty-handed to the cashier at the bar whereupon rested a copy of *Provincia*, the largest daily newspaper in the state.

"Can I take a look?"

"You can have it," she said.

My eyes were pulled to the Style section – Estilo – and photographs of huge paintings on exhibit opening night at a local gallery, Espacio Arte Contemporaneo. The paintings were stunning in black and white, and in front of them, colorfully dressed and coiffed and made-up, stood groups of notably engaged people. Clearly, this show was generating heat. And I resolved to see it.

Passing through bright green trees in the park across from the hotel, I entered the Museo de Arte Contemporaneo, showed the article to three employees and asked for directions, checked out their exhibit of original paintings from twentieth century Mexican calendars, and soon received a hand-drawn map to a place only several blocks away. In an affluent neighborhood in front of a modern one-story house converted into a gallery, I exited the taxi and glanced at a large empty birdcage, and moving toward the building saw some enormous exotic birds in cages, and walked inside to be riveted by the face – more than six feet high and almost five across – of a mustachioed old man wearing a white hat.

"That's really good," I said to the middle-aged man who greeted me.

"Gracias."

"What's the artist's name?"

"Fernando Motilla Zarur."

"I saw his picture in the paper. How old is he?"

Paint it Blue

"Eighteen."

My mouth popped open. "Eighteen?" That's like someone his age pitching in the Major Leagues.

"He's my son."

At that point, having heard praise in imperfect Spanish, the young and slender Fernando Motilla modestly entered the room and shook my hand.

"Can I ask you a few questions?"

"Sure," he said.

* * *

Fernando Motilla had always been an indifferent and thoroughly average student until he entered junior high school. Then he became a poor student. History induced yawns. Math irritated him. Science was excruciating. Only his drawing class stimulated him, but it met once a week for an hour, and Motilla never considered restraining himself until the next official artistic opportunity. He sketched fellow students in his history classes, and drew still lifes while teachers droned about equations, and with quick strokes crafted landscapes to overwhelm grim recitations of the internal organs of frogs. His teachers, often having assumed the lad was a diligent even frenetic note-taker, were unimpressed upon discovering the nature of his output.

"You're not studying," some declared, hovering over his desk to grab his work and wad it into balls hurled into wastebaskets.

"Don't draw in class," others admonished before snatching his efforts and tearing them up.

A few teachers were less theatrical and spoke only in writing at report-card time, handing Motilla his usual six out of ten, equivalent to a D.

Regardless of professorial response, Motilla remained unflustered. He knew he would soon make more drawings. Their creation was a natural urge, an expression of passion that nothing else evoked. His parents understood. They'd received his artwork as gifts since he was five and always urged him to develop his talent. Now it was the year two thousand, Fernando had just turned fourteen, and the ambitious family made a decision: he would quit school, take art classes, and paint full-time.

Painters often make their earliest efforts in landscapes, which are useful in developing technique but not creatively demanding – Motilla thus began studying with Augustín Torres, and painted mountains and lakes and oceans, and soon made his first sale, for two thousand pesos, about two hundred dollars. When Motilla was fifteen, Torres publicly declared he was the first student who'd ever surpassed him. The teacher also expressed his sentiments in writing: "You're beginning your artistic life. Enjoy it because everyone isn't an artist. Consider yourself privileged."

Fernando Motilla understood the opportunity and embraced studies in surrealism with Rafael Flores. Classes were held downtown in La Casa de Cultura, a huge stone colonial fusion of church and fort. Inside these impressive walls Motilla and the other students painted the human form, generally that of a naked young woman – for centuries the most exalted subject of artists, Jesus Christ not withstanding. The young painter was growing. He discovered Dali and Magritte, champions of surrealism from Spain and Belgium.

"You probably also love Diego Rivera and Frida Kahlo," I said of Mexico's greatest and most glamorous painter, respectively.

"Not really. I don't like their themes, but I like their color, composition, and technique. I'd seen their work every day since childhood, so I suppose they began to bore me."

No one is aware of every influence, and in this case Motilla does not realize what he learned from the exotic, often ill, frequently intoxicated but always intriguing Frida Kahlo who with paint powerfully depicted her physical and psychic pain: some of the most compelling images are of her fractured spine and pelvis. One of Motilla's first two sales of surrealism was *Life and Death* which perches a skull atop a body that is normal except for an exposed spine and pelvis. Frida would've liked it; Diego would've bought it.

"You should ask a thousand dollars for those paintings," Rafael Flores told Motilla.

"That's way too much."

"No, it's very low."

The teacher was correct. Both paintings sold for a grand. The astute collector was Michoacán's secretary of government. He also offered the precocious fifteen-year old a chance to go to Italy for intensive study. Motilla elected to stay with his family and, under Miguel Rincón, study a variety of abstract techniques. He used sand, pigment, and encaustic materials, and began painting much larger works. Though the soft-spoken Motilla is by all appearances quite different than the depressed, alcoholic, and ultimately suicidal Jackson Pollock, king of the drip painters, he feels an artistic kinship.

"Dali started surrealism, and Pollock, by flinging paint onto canvases, invented painting in action. After brushing on an acrylic foundation, sometimes with representational elements, I'd put my fingers into paint then let it drop onto the canvas. I learned a lot about the atmosphere of color and texture. But after less than ten paintings I thought that's enough of the abstract. It's possible I'll return to it someday."

At age sixteen Motilla arrived at another crossroads: he quit taking regular art classes, wanting to eliminate the influence of his teachers. They'd taught him a lot but by working alone he sensed he'd grow more artistically; his intuition proved accurate, and he's already had three solo exhibitions and earned critical praise, substantial publicity, and a growing group of public and private collectors who now pay three thousand dollars for the paintings in the current show – *Retratos Pluriemociales* (Portraits of Different States of Mind).

"Let me show you," said Motilla, leading a tour into each of the gallery's several rooms with tile floors. "I've tried to capture their moods at the moments I took their pictures."

We examined "hyper-realistic" portraits of numerous happy or introspective people – young adult female friends, children of associates, a former teacher, his grandmother, his mother, and sister. An open-mouthed Austrian woman is so animated she seems ready to gnaw her way out of the canvas. As we entered the hall, the atmosphere changed: an intense man glares at everyone through a large left eye and an alarming, half-closed right eye.

"There's a guy that's tough to deal with," I said.

"That's my dad."

"Oh – of course. Now I see. I like the technique here, more emotional, not photorealistic. And the heavy application of paint is effective."

"That's impasto. I used the same technique with my grandfather."

"I notice some of the pictures are very clear and some are foggy or a little out of focus."

"Right. We call these works unfocused. I sketch the portrait beforehand – as with all the others – but with these I use a compressor to spray the paint on a little at a time. The process is aerógrafo."

"How long does it take to do these?"

"All of them take about two weeks."

"I see there's another guy not too happy. That's you. Are you angry?"

"More not satisfied. I was painting my emotions."

Father Juan Motilla had joined the conversation several times and now did so again. He'd owned a construction company and other businesses in San Luis Potosí, in central Mexico, before bringing the family further south to Morelia several years ago.

"Now I just sell birds and paintings," he said.

"You're obviously very supportive of Fernando's career."

"Absolutely. Fernando and I know he can't rest because in order to climb the mountain, you can't limit yourself. If he rests, he'll regress."

"I agree. Let's see some new work."

Father and son led me back to Fernando's office. That's where we entered another world, as one does with fine music and movies. We entered the surreal world of *Mujer Golfista* – Lady Golfer. A sleek lady in a chic dress reveals her bare back to you, holding the driver straight up as she peers into beckoning yet forbidding all-white eternity. The golf ball is teed high and ready to drive. You can hit it if you want. *Mujer Golfista* never will. She'll forever be the pensive and motionless star in a significant work by young Fernando Motilla.

Distress in Polanco

Penelope, an art gallery owner in Houston, and Clyde, a building contractor, married two months after meeting last year, fueled by lust and undeterred by different interests. Penelope detested football and baseball, so Clyde never insisted she watch either in person or on TV. Clyde didn't understand contemporary art but graciously attended most opening night parties at the gallery and, save the first time, didn't call people on canvas deformed and the abstracts spaghetti.

The marriage proceeded satisfactorily and Clyde agreed to accompany Penelope to Mexico City where she was scouting two artists and planning to introduce her husband to elegant, tree-blessed Polanco where Penelope had several times enjoyed an intimate museum honoring great muralist David Alfaro Siqueiros and indie films at Casa del Arte, four subterranean theaters topped by a lively street-side restaurant and bar whose patrons, though unpretentious, exuded wealth and sophistication.

On a peaceful Polanco street featuring seven-figure residences that must be purchased in cash dollars, their taxi parked in front of a sleek space lightened inside by much glass on its façade. After buying two tickets Penelope told her husband, "Siqueiros' portrait of his wife is perhaps the finest such work I've seen. It's over there, at the top of the staircase. We'll walk right into her enormous beautiful face."

They instead looked up at a blank wall behind the stairs.

"Where's his wife?" Penelope demanded in Spanish.

"She's being restored," an employee replied.

"What's wrong with her?"

The employee shrugged.

"Where are some of his other paintings and your exhibitions by other artists?"

We really don't have any paintings up right now, but we do have a special exhibition around the corner and a film over there."

Around the corner there were piles of bricks next to shattered walls. Penelope and Clyde only glanced at the wall paragraph noting something about the artists building a site-specific structure, dining there, and then demolishing it. Siqueiros would've shot those guys.

The couple then heard strange unidentifiable sounds and opened black curtains to behold a movie screen that featured garbage being flung, by a person or people off-screen, onto an expanse of refuse.

"We better go see one of your movies," Clyde said.

They walked to a main street and waved at a taxi.

"To Casa del Arte," Penelope said.

"What?"

"Your great theaters on Anatoly France near the corner of Presidente Masaryk."

The cabbie silently drove to the location.

"Where is it?" she said, lunging out of the car while Clyde paid, and marched into the building.

"Where's Casa del Arte?" she asked a uniformed man relaxing in the dim and dusty remains of the restaurant.

"They closed."

"When?"

"About a year ago."

"Why?"

"The economy. And technology for home movies."

"People in Polanco have plenty of money to pay to watch top films in a theater."

The man smiled.

Penelope pulled Clyde's hand, led him outside, and spoke to an older gentleman on the sidewalk. "I can't believe people in Polanco stopped supporting independent films."

"They may not have," he said. "The owner sold the theaters to a guy who's building a bowling alley."

"Too bad that's not finished," Clyde said. "Let's find a bullfight."

Crime Without Punishment

I don't mind Rocio Caballero paints me in *Lesson 9: Omnipotence*. I'm not ashamed to be a powerful man. I'm proud to sit in my vast slaughterhouse surrounded by hanging corpses of skinned and gutted cows. My dark tailored suit matches the fur of an unskinned cow on the floor where it and other cows wait for the knife that skinned two pig heads, every slice making me wealthier and happier holding my cigar and contemplating a world I control.

I'm quite enjoying this whole exhibition, *Crime Without Punishment*, at Museo del Pueblo in Guanajuato. And I'm edified to see what happens to those less formidable. Look at that dead rabbit. His big left eye is right on you as you little notice two deceased birds next to the rabbit because you're stunned *The Feast* also presents a man in red tie and suspenders who was caught wearing the face of a bear and had to be eliminated.

Far more in common I have with *Noa* the big game hunter relaxing barefoot and in red tie as he sits on a red sofa next to a little dog under three grand trophies, a rhino, a deer, and a bear, high on the wall over small drawings of animals he's yet to kill and drawings on the sofa he's yet to post near blank paper he's yet to draw on.

Ah, that could have been me in *Lesson 20: Forever a Beau III*. Frankly, that could still be me, albeit in younger form. This handsome fellow in suit and red tie bears merely a sword-skewered medallion of his heart for he has broken the chain of love though it manacles his right wrist in front of a wall of crimson hearts of those who loved and still love him. Who are they? They're everyone, scrawled on the wall: Kara, Cora, Cecilia, Bety, Maru, and even Diego, Alex, and Julio. No need to further recite. The beau will write countless new names after pinning crimson hearts on the rough wooden wall.

I'm going to join those eleven fellows in *Dissertations from Great Height*. They're sitting on a horizontal steel beam above a vast city of monuments and skyscrapers and freeways. They look quite nice in slacks and red ties and especially masks of a donkey, a rabbit, a pig, a wolf, a monkey and more beasts they'll either emulate or kill, probably both as the feline man in the middle cuts white paper into connected people floating or perhaps falling to the great city.

The title painting, *Crime Without Punishment*, is painted from above four men in fine suits and red ties relaxing on circular stone stairs, scissors in right hands cutting white paper figures of people strewn on steps, how happy they are, a pig, a dog, a cat, and a bird on stairs spiraling down, I'm guessing, to hell.

Picasso

George Thomas Clark

Franco Beholds Guernica

I'm no longer angry with Pablo Picasso though I should be. His most famous work, and perhaps the most powerful of the twentieth century, *Guernica*, is celebrated as a denunciation of war, particularly when hostilities result in deaths of civilians. I absolutely agree. I swear I didn't order the attack on the Republican stronghold of Guernica in northern Spain in April 1937. What I believe happened is that the communist Republicans dynamited the town and then burned it before fleeing. I'm shocked our German allies proudly explained how they conducted the attack. If the Germans really were responsible, then they struck without my knowledge or approval. Even during our Civil War, I loved Spain too much to allow the destruction of a beautiful Basque town.

For more than thirty years *Guernica* had resided primarily in New York, at the Museum of Modern Art, but I showed goodwill by offering to bring this national treasure home to Spain. Picasso wouldn't allow this until his Spain, which he'd abandoned in his late teens at the turn of the century, had a government he approved of and that allowed "public liberties and democratic institutions." In the real world, outside art studios, I understood Divine Providence had sent me to execute thousands of communists and other enemies, and after the war to suppress, imprison, or kill those who threatened our strong new government.

As a sensitive and creative man I mourned the passing of Picasso in 1973 and hope he would've regretted my death two years later. We're Spain's two greatest heroes, and I stand today in the Reina Sofia Museum in Madrid and admire not a denunciation of my Nationalist forces and me but an evocative painting about the tragedy of war. As a lifelong military man, and once the youngest general in all of Europe, I understand combat far better than most. I therefore appreciate the power of this massive work more than eleven feet by twenty-five, and am impressed that it's flanked by two seated security guards, though I'm worried they're unarmed and women, who should be nurturing the young at home.

In crowds gathered in front of *Guernica* throughout the day, no one recognized me as I repeatedly returned to gaze at the wailing woman on the left clutching her dead baby, and the bull above her with a fiery tail, and below her the shrieking and dying soldier on the ground, broken sword in hand. In picture center, under a lamp burning like malicious sun, a horse bellows through an open mouth with spiked tongue. Further right two ghost-like creatures stretch to look on in fright. And on the right border a woman extends both arms and cries to heavens waiting with fire. This painting I certainly would've brought home and am delighted it returned several years after I departed.

Tame Her

Francoise's much taller and lovelier than I and forty years younger losing control and I am too but mustn't let her know. The following night as she envelops me I pinch and pull her breasts and thrust my hand and bite her neck and scratch with my whiskers and huff like a bull she'll never forget.

Don't think I'd ever get permanently attached to you, I say. Don't think you mean anything to me. I like independence. You're like all women either goddesses or door mats and tonight you're the latter. Nobody has any real importance to me. People are like little grains of dust floating in sunlight. I need only push with a broom, I say, and then caress her again. A few days later I press a lit cigarette to her cheek. I expect a cry, a retreat. Instead, she's doesn't flinch and I pull away and say this isn't a good idea, I may want to look at you again.

Francoise Gilot must accept I have other women, some from the past others the future. She knows Dora Maar must be constantly available. I rarely show up any more but she must be ready. Dora's a weakling I detest and think Francoise's becoming like that too. She needs my presence to feel like a woman. She needs my energy to breathe. She can't endure without me. None of them can.

When Francoise complains about Dora one evening I jerk her to the edge of the Seine and threaten to throw her in. This is my right and so is trying to seduce her friends. I am Picasso and still her master. She doesn't want young men. She's got me, when I want. And now, at last, I do and insist she live with me. If she doesn't I may use this belt in my hand.

She loves being around genius and watches me stare at canvases for two or three hours. I may brush on some paint or move to others in my large studio where I work early afternoon to late night. It's torturous, yet people believe my talent makes everything easy. I'm being eaten up by an ulcer that worsens the harder I work. It's probably cancer. No one cares. That's why I'm so unhappy. My painting is going badly. I may have to visit Dora, but primarily for talk. Maria-Therese is the one I prefer in bed. Francoise must compete for my affection. I love the tension. So do my women. To satisfy me, they must be tense and passionate.

Paint it Blue

I have so many troubles they must help me forget. Look at my son Paulo. He's a lazy alcoholic who tears things up and the police blame me. I shouldn't be responsible. People always expect me to resolve matters. They think I can paint money. They don't know how difficult my life is. I need to relax more. After several years with Francoise I realize she, and our young son and daughter, are smothering me so I travel without them for business or bullfights. It's my affair what I do and with whom. I'm tired of her crying and pleading. She's weak and bores me. I don't know why I let her stay. She won't leave. She's addicted like the others. She's not going to end it. She'd be terrified without me. I may be in my seventies but am still Picasso and romancing women all over the south of France. That will make Francoise understand. She can't leave me. I may kill myself if she does.

If that will make you happier, I better not attempt to stop you, she says.

George Thomas Clark

Electrician Receives Picassos

During my career as an electrician and handyman extraordinaire in southern France, I wired, painted, and repaired the chateaus and farmhouses of many distinguished people, and my favorite was Pablo Picasso. It's been almost forty years, but through the mist I recall installing a burglar alarm at one of his farm houses and fixing up some of his other places. He loved my work. And he appreciated my clever but gentle repartee. One day, struggling to stand – he was in his nineties – Picasso said, "Pierre Le Guennec, I've created thousands of great works of art, thrilled everyone from aesthetes to simpletons the world over, made countless millions of dollars, and bedded hundreds of beautiful young women. I shan't live much longer, and I've already given my heirs far too much. Will you please take these two hundred seventy-one pieces of art as symbols of my appreciation for the electronic security and good fellowship you've provided?"

I could not turn the old fellow down. Indeed, I recall building the wooden crates that delightful day. And I took them to my slightly-tilted two-story home and just let them rest in my garage until an afternoon a few weeks ago when I tripped over one of the crates and fell face first onto the other that bloodied my prominent Gallic nose. I shouted epithets I dare not repeat in French and that you wouldn't understand anyway. Then I picked up a handy axe, which I had used to demolish many unsightly walls I soon skillfully replaced, and began striking both crates until I realized the danger and ceased swinging so I could grab a long screwdriver, my scalpel, if you will, and deftly open both crates and ensure that the sketches, paintings, and collages therein were undamaged. I ran to awaken my wife from her daily nap, and together we decided it was time to get those old boxes out of the way and authenticate our property since we're getting old, in our early seventies, and would like to pass this on to our kids.

I thought Picasso's son Claude would be thrilled to see so many of the master's unknown works and anxious to help me. Instead, the greedy lout, who's always had money rained on him by his father's estate, called the police. They not only impounded my collection but raided my house to look for more Picassos. They didn't find any.

Paint it Blue

Everything I had was in those boxes. Some experts say the works may be worth about eighty millions dollars. That's why they keep pestering me: "Why would Picasso give an electrician such prizes? You weren't his friend. He never mentioned you. And he never wrote a single word about you. No one knows you." Okay, perhaps it was his wife, Jacqueline Roque, who gave me the art. And she certainly wouldn't have done so if Picasso hadn't wanted her to. Don't look at me that way. I suppose it's possible I found the stuff in a box amid all my wood and tools. I can't remember. I may have found everything in the garbage. I don't know why he didn't sign and date the works. He was old. He gave all this to me. I'm not a thief. Ask my wife.

George Thomas Clark

Picasso Sparkles

I first ask then urge directors at the de Young Museum in San Francisco to let me in two hours early so characters in *Picasso, Masterpieces from the Musée National Picasso, Paris* can relax and speak to me before hordes enter and distract them. The directors ultimately agree, and at seven thirty in the morning I descend into the galleries and first stop in front of *Woman with a Cataract*, and right after I smile she says, "Don't ogle my left eye."

I assure her I'm not, that I'm looking into both.

"No one examines an artistically conventional old woman unless she glows from a dead eye," she says.

Quietly I move on.

When I approach the head and torso of a roughneck in *Self-Portrait*, he says, "Trust me, I'm nude from the waist down. I'm only twenty-five and virile and must be ready. My girlfriend Fernande Olivier's hot and when I don't do her someone else does. I confront her but she says she can do whatever I do. And I suppose she can, if I don't lock her in the studio. That's the best place for her after we've smoked opium."

"Come here," says a pretty young lady with silken black hair in *Portrait of Olga in an Armchair*. "You're a witness. Picasso thinks I'm beautiful and paints me so, in an elegant dress as I sit in embroidered space, holding an ornate fan. I don't look bored but serene. I'm regal not materialistic. I'm not bourgeois but chic. I should be. I need more money. I deserve it. I'm his wife. In 1921 we have a son. Picasso should stop painting strange forms and concentrate on classical beauty. And he must stay away from Maria-Therese Walter. She's a teenage whore when they meet, and several years later their daughter's a bitch, and I leave but don't go away. I follow them and shout what's going on. His treachery's destroying my health."

"Try to stay beautiful as you are, in 1918, and don't move forward," I say.

The domestic life of Picasso is good for books and movies as well as paintings but for awhile I want only the latter and approach *Seated Woman* who says, "Amazing my huge hands and feet on canvas are sexy like the huge arms and legs of *Two Women Running on the Beach*. They're joyful exposing their left breasts moving fast hair flying back as the long left arm of one propels them into paradise. Go on, chase them."

I demur, and walk toward *The Acrobat* and after I study him a minute he says, "I don't really have a spine I have the junction of an arm and leg forming my ass while that hand and foot caress the ground on one side and my other leg reaches back over my face and also onto the ground, making me the most flexible man in the world."

I know *Figures at the Seashore* won't talk to me. Angry at eternal interruptions they shed traditional human form and entangle themselves exchanging sharp tongues as they detach her breasts and place them pointing high on her open left thigh. They're a striking couple, angular, other-worldly, and unapproachable.

What a lovely and flowing and fertile creature Maria-Therese Walter is in *Reading*, I think and then tell her.

"Yes, he also thinks so several years and we have a daughter but go over and look how he uses me in *The Farmer's Wife*. I don't like to analyze his work, especially when I'm the subject, and hope he isn't using me as a symbol of European 'complacency...during the Spanish Civil War.' I'm afraid in this case his attack is far more personal and I can't avoid insight: he's put me flabby on my back, a grimacing, grumpy woman who's just been screwed by a rooster who's bit a hole in my navel and pounced between my shaved legs. I still love Picasso but don't want to marry him."

"I know you'll respond you do everything for art but I must tell you *The Farmer's Wife* is a malicious stroke," I tell Picasso in *Self-Portrait in Straw Hat*.

"Not malicious but perceptive," he says. "Look at me now. I'm a cockeyed wretch with a blue face and wild looking as Van Gogh. That's emotional truth and what I paint."

In photos Dora Maar appears serene and beautiful and at least is the latter in *Portrait of Dora Maar* but I suspect serene she's not because of unmatched eyes and nostrils in a painting that captures psychic rather than physical reality. "No, you're not hallucinating but perhaps Picasso is and I know I sometimes am," she says. "I'm sad and angry and depressed and that's why Picasso calls me *The Weeping Woman* and paints me that way the same year, and in 1939 portrays me heavier and more distorted and smoldering before outburst, and maybe I should blame his cruelty but don't always and after he leaves I undergo psychoanalysis which is something he definitely needs as well."

Francoise Gilot, in an iconic magazine photo, projects strength and independence as she marches ahead of Picasso who dutifully carries a huge umbrella shielding her from the sun on a beach in the south of France. That woman is absent in *The Shadow* from which Picasso says, "I know it's a weak and maudlin painting because that's what I am now, a mere morbid black shadow looming over the dreary image of a lover, and mother of my two youngest children, who's abandoned me."

"Don't shoot," I shout at soldiers armored, shielded, and pointing their rifles at women and children in *Massacre in Korea*.

They swing their guns around to aim at me, and one asks, "You want it, instead?"

I look at women naked and pregnant holding children and caring for babies and a pubescent daughter, and know I should do something but am afraid and can't speak and duck away.

"I'm a sentinel I'm a muse I'm everything for Picasso as you can see," says Jacquline Roque in *Jacqueline with Crossed Hands*. "My face is chiseled, strong and determined and I'm eternally ready to protect my man. By 1969 when Picasso's almost ninety I engulf him with arms and lips in *The Kiss*, my eyes looking ever up to him while his huge black ones glaze toward eternity."

Vincent

George Thomas Clark

She Lives with Vincent

As oldest of ten children of a porter, I clean houses and make clothes, and Mother works by my side and younger siblings too. This isn't enough, though, and we go to soup kitchens and anywhere else for help until I decide to sell what I have and men like it well enough, and I bear three children by customers I can't name and one daughter survives and I'm thirty-one and pregnant again when I meet Vincent in 1882.

He tells me I've been ploughed by life but appreciates that because he has too and needs someone who won't reject him like his widowed cousin Kee and art dealers and his parents who curse him for living with me. Vincent isn't going to listen to them. I'm the only woman he doesn't have to pay in cash, and he's thankful to give my daughter and me and soon my son a place to live and says life is so much better waking up next to me.

He sketches me all the time but I tell him, you'll never make anything doing that, nobody wants to look at me especially the strange way you draw and paint.

I'm learning, I'm getting close, you'll see, everyone will.

I can't see his hobby going anywhere. After all, he's being supported by his brother. I don't want to lie around all day while he scribbles. I go back to cleaning and sewing and as usual earn little so again entertain men while Vincent cries and Theo rushes to The Hague and says, get rid of Sien Hoornik or she'll ruin your career.

That's a lie. I'm good for Vincent's work, even if it brings in nothing. Look at me in *Sien, Sewing, Half-Figure,* I'm a diligent woman making clothes and more money than Vincent ever does painting. Sure, I'm unattractive and worn and weak-chinned, but Vincent isn't any better. We're what people like us can expect to find and both quite unhappy and Vincent more so than I even in *Sorrow* when I sit, burying my face in weary arms as breasts sink onto thighs in a horrible world.

Fine, Vincent, I say when he insists on leaving, in 1883, you'll never have anyone like us again, my daughter loves you, the baby boy thinks you're his father, you and I may not be in love but we have each other, and you'll never have anyone again.

I don't wish Vincent bad luck, but I know him, and am not

surprised to hear he shoots himself in 1890. I know he has to do it. And I'm sure he would understand in 1904 I'm fifty-four and married to a no good man and can no longer sell myself and, feeling like an old whore, jump into a river. I'm telling you, Vincent should've stayed with me.

George Thomas Clark

The Potato Eaters

May I join you, please? I know I've caught you starting dinner, and it looks delicious. I love potatoes, too. May I have some? Oh, don't worry, I'll pay. I know you have little enough. But you have company and a warm home.

No, I don't know Vincent, not personally, but believe me, he isn't making fun of you. He respects you and appreciates your difficulties. That's why he prepared studies before painting this scene. He wants people to enter your lives.

But you feel he's portrayed you as simple and ugly. That's not what he means. I assure you, Vincent knows all of you would've flourished if raised in a family that provided books and education and opportunities. You're not to blame. Vincent isn't blaming anyone. It's fate. And it's not a bad one.

That's right, you don't want to be Vincent, God help him, and you don't want to be any of his relatives, and you don't want to be me. You're happier than all of us. I agree. Please let me have a cup of coffee, or is it tea? Thank you.

Listen, in my truck outside – it's like a big wagon with an engine – I have some delicacies I think you'll like. May I?

I begin dashing outside and back, carrying trays of potatoes roasted, baked, boiled, scalloped, mashed and French fried, and smothered in various combinations of bacon, cheese, sour cream, garlic, broccoli and many spices. Here you are. Please, try these. What do you think? You love them. Fantastic. Would it be all right if Vincent joins us? He's never had anything like this either.

Disaster at Norton Simon

Norton Simon mastered business while young but not until age forty-seven did he begin to voraciously hunt art and acquire stellar works by Rubens, Rembrandt, Degas, Van Gogh, and Picasso as well as many other titans starting in the fourteenth century. His collection at the Norton Simon Museum, in this shady, sedate, and exclusive community, is aesthetically priceless and worth billions on the market, yet many convenience stores offer a more robust security profile. One cannot count on the bored and disheartened employees, uniformed in tired blazers, who stand all day, watching visitors look at paintings. Perhaps they'd be motivated if armed but, alas, they are neither. I hope at least one person at the museum bore a firearm last Friday. If so, he must have been on break in the basement or dozing in his car

He couldn't have been in the galleries where at first I thought Hollywood was shooting a movie: a bearded young man with the wild eyes of Rasputin was hyperventilating before *David Slaying Goliath*, the masterpiece by Peter Paul Rubens. Even in the presence of one of the world's greatest paintings, art lovers are generally able to stand in a self-controlled manner and admire dashing David's rosy right cheek matching his red garments, and marvel at the man's musculature – forget tiny underdog; this David's an all pro linebacker – and envision the circular swoop, from the sword cocked behind his head, down through the already battered and bleeding head, under David's foot, of poor Goliath. Measuring more than four feet high and three wide plus ornate frame, this painting has been a sensation since completion in 1616. For the frightening fellow, whose panting and gesticulating drove those near the work away, and deterred others from approaching, *David Slaying Goliath* was a symbol of profound allure and abject survival: repeatedly he lunged toward the painting, almost pressing his nose to the canvas, then jumped back and exhaled, "Aaahhh." After a couple of minutes – time is difficult to reckon during stressful events – he grabbed the frame high, a hand on each side just below the level of David's head, and pulled. The painting stayed but an alarm erupted. And I believe I heard a meek, "Please, sir," from one of the uniformed employees.

Looking like Goliath about to be smitten, Rasputin dashed out of this gallery and turned right and bulldozed into the nineteenth century section straight to its jewel, *Portrait of a Peasant (Patience Escalier)* by Vincent van Gogh. Most patrons in the museum had gathered a prudent distance from the man who, standing close, bored into tormented eyes of the peasant then popped back to stare at the jagged and horrifying blue background, a world of dread around the peasant's incandescent yellow hat that scorches his beaten face and casts terrible illumination onto his tattered turquoise coat.

"Sir, please, come with me," said the young man who'd sold me my ticket and ventured out from the counter.

Rasputin reached into his worn coat, far less glamorous than the peasant's immortal rag, and retrieved a pistol which he pointed at the lad, who froze wide-eyed and clearly expected to die, but the lunatic turned instead on the peasant and shot out his left eye, eliciting shrieks, then his right. He pivoted, and through a rapidly parting sea of patrons, ran out the entrance. Once summoned, the police hastily arrived at this prominent location on busy Colorado Boulevard. There was no need for an ambulance. The hundred-million-dollar peasant will have to be operated on by art restoration experts who that evening were summoned from the Van Gogh Museum in Holland, land of the artist's birth. The assailant is still at large. And the Norton Simon Museum is doubtless contemplating enhanced security measures.

Woman Rips Irises

"Why're you staring at *Irises*?" a woman asked.

"Beg your pardon," I replied, spinning to see no one in the Getty Museum gallery of impressionism. Perplexed, I turned and again studied undulating knife-green flowers, topped by morose blue buds, Vincent van Gogh had painted while he battled mental illness at Saint-Rémy asylum, wishing he were better or dead.

"You prefer joyless flowers to me, Cezanne's *Young Italian Woman at a Table*," she said.

"Not necessarily. I didn't realize we'd be talking. But since we are, I must respectfully say you're rather dour today and every time I've seen you. Try looking at me, and the thousands who visit every year. Take your face out of your hand and your elbow off that table. Stand up straight. And smile."

"Those are presumptuous remarks. I've nothing to smile about."

"Why not?"

She didn't reply. She didn't move.

Van Goghs Argue

For reasons of physical and emotional safety I try to avoid family conflicts, which always harm those involved and frequently damage anyone else in range. Such unpleasantness was far from mind last week as I entered Norton Simon Museum. A safe and soothing afternoon among master painters I would surely have.

After purchasing my ticket I strolled to one of the great works in art – *Portrait of a Peasant (Patience Escalier)* – and stood close to examine the old gardener's sunny yellow hat burning a face worn and sad yet stoic and dignified.

"Stand back," I heard, and turned but no one was nearby except the debauched gardener encircled by violent dark blue brushstrokes. "Are you a fool? Dozens of times every day I'm disgusted by people staring and commenting, 'Look at that ugly self-portrait of Van Gogh. I don't want my picture taken with him.' I guarantee no one ever saw me like this till I posed for Van Gogh."

"Shut up, you lout," said the painting to the Peasant's immediate right – *The Mulberry Tree*. The branches and leaves weren't really branches and leaves but writhing snakes ready to strike. "You're to blame. At the nearby asylum in Saint Rémy, everyone hoped Vincent would improve and paint pretty scenes of the countryside, but the trauma of studying and painting a frightening peasant induced epileptic attacks."

"I'm getting my axe," said the peasant.

"Not when my branches wrap around your neck."

"Quiet, both of you," said the dear old lady in *Portrait of Artist's Mother*, to the right of the tree. "Small wonder you torment Vincent. Look at the serene light-green face my son has given me. He knows I'm stable and caring and not at all responsible for his distress."

From the opposite wall a female – *Head of a Peasant Woman in White Bonnet* – ordered, "Get over here."

I turned and walked across the gallery to face a tough woman with broad nose and dull eyes under a cavernous white bonnet.

"History calls me a peasant because that's what Vincent felt," she said. "He was selfish and strange and didn't appreciate what I offered. Maybe I would've appeared haggard and spent even if I hadn't posed for Vincent, but not so soon. I'm just thankful he painted me in Holland before his paintings got crazy in France."

Straight over her a liquor bottle in *Still Life* stated, "I could've saved Vincent."

"Drinking alcohol and absinthe damaged Vincent," I said.

"I don't represent alcohol even if Vincent thought I did. I am the embodiment of modern psychopharmacology. The brown bowl holding a white vase to my right and the bottle and white bowl on the other side suggest not a mundane table scene but an apothecary and the implements of inspired pain management. If Vincent could've taken what he painted, he'd have been all right."

George Thomas Clark

Starry Night

during day
they hate
me in town
they won't
tonight i
paint solar
stars burning
my eyes

Sunflowers

I don't feel well. In fact I'm dizzy and weak and in danger of vomiting. I shouldn't have taken this vacation. I should've stayed home and recovered from ulcers and a still-undiagnosed nervous disorder. I felt I could recover if I relaxed in Europe and immersed myself in culture and met some enchanting women. I think that's realistic but on the flight a mere plastic glass of red wine assaults my stomach and I stagger down the aisle into one of those dreadful vibrating bathrooms. In my condition I pray I'll simply pass out and into the hereafter but my body doesn't cooperate and I have to return to my seat for a flight that seems to Mars.

In Amsterdam, despite ministrations of a doctor and fine food delivered to my bedside, I suffer two days in my hotel before rising and taking a taxi to the shrine of creative endeavor, the Riksmuseum Vincent van Gogh. In late afternoon I enter in reasonable shape but am soon in a haze and quite confused and compelled to dash through a door and into a stall where I faint.

How long have I been out? It must be hours. The bathroom's dark like a closet and I can't see which way to go until flicking my lighter. I ease and stumble down a hall into a gallery alight with something more powerful than any fire: *Vase with Fourteen Sunflowers.* Lord, what a feast for eyes and balm for the soul. I stare. I breathe. I yearn. And I note the quite devastating return of stomach and head pains.

I should've first stopped to buy some of Amersterdam's renowned marijuana but at least I have fire and rolling papers and, before me, the finest alternative in the world. Several times I pinch the tallest sunflower, noting it's perfectly dry, and roll a tight joint and inhale sedative delight until Vincent, in a self-portrait nearby, summons me and says, let me have a toke, then try the lighter yellow sunflower on your far left.

The new stuff also enchants and, as Vincent directs, so does the flower with a black center, and another with red, and one in blue, and I'm thrilled he emerges from his frame, strides to the sunflowers, rips them from their vase, flings onto the floor, and chugs something from the vase he'd long ago signed pretty blue Vincent.

George Thomas Clark

Van Gogh v. Gauguin

I didn't want to go to Arles but Vincent kept writing that by painting side by side and sharing artistic ideas we could create our finest works. Really, I had no other offers in October 1888 so relented and took paint and canvases to the south of France and moved into the yellow house that Vincent had been touting as a crucible of creation soon to also become our art gallery.

He'd been painting a lot and his work was pretty good but soon I said, "Look here, Vincent, you're working too much in the moment and need to paint more from memory so your mind can further develop what you've seen."

He tried some my way before saying, "Paul, my mind cannot capture the passion as well as my eyes which at any rate are connected to my mind which is on fire and the reason I'm painting starry nights and sunflowers and landscapes and vineyards and my rocking chair and yours and my portraits and others and creating so fast and well, I believe, that you should pay more attention and respect me. I need your emotional support to be safe in night cafés where I may 'ruin myself, go mad, or commit a crime.'"

"You're disturbed, Vincent. Go to bed. I'm heading for the brothel."

"I'll come, too."

"No you won't."

"I must."

"The girls are afraid of you, Vincent. They don't want to see you and will certainly never screw you again. And they won't talk to me anymore if I'm with you."

"Stupid whores. Don't let them influence you."

"I'm leaving."

I turned to the door, and a slender but exceptionally strong left hand grabbed my left bicep and whipped me around to receive a right hand to the jaw that knocked me back into the door.

"Paul, forgive me, please. You're a bastard but a saint."

Moving both hands like wheels I carefully approached Vincent, who extended hands, presumably in supplication, but I wasn't presuming what this deranged man would do, and threw several wild punches that missed until I relaxed against a man not fighting back and hit him a right to the jaw and left to the temple and right to his left kidney as he fell.

In the brothel I drank fast and screwed hard and felt good again when Vincent staggered in, pouring blood from his ear and holding a paper soaked red he presented to one of the ladies and said, "Please keep this. I love all of you and the whole world even though it loathes my work and me."

George Thomas Clark

Vincent's Self-Portraits

George Thomas Clark – Vincent, I think you're tired of painting peasants, that you want subjects more perceptive, more learned, and that's why in 1886 you start painting yourself.

Vincent van Gogh – I never look down on peasants. They fascinate me.

GTC – But you've exchanged them for the most riveting face in the history of art – your own.

VVG – I merely look for something that moves me and that I think I can understand or at least interpret.

GTC – In *Self-Portrait with Dark Felt Hat* you appear stable, content, even bourgeois.

VVG – I do have moments of relative tranquility. I think in this self-portrait, perhaps my first in paint, I allow myself to fantasize, to tell something a little better than the truth.

GTC – You soon become much more candid in your two works titled *Self-Portrait with Pipe.*

VVG – I sense if I can look in the mirror long enough, if I can endure that, I can paint what I'm feeling, what I feel now, what I've always felt: tension, loneliness, desperation, looming insanity.

GTC – Those problems you begin to portray quite well in the Paris spring of 1887. You're stern, frightening, and miserable.

VVG – I can be little else. So I paint.

GTC – Most artists filter their feelings. And the few who try to be candid can't really convey what they feel, and what they feel isn't as compelling as what you feel.

VVG – Sometimes I hate my work as much as those who mock or ignore me.

GTC – That's changing, even in 1887, people are noticing, artists, dealers.

VVG – Then they should buy something.

GTC – Indeed. In this summer of 1887 you seem, by van Gogh standards, if I may, to be only intense and introspective. But soon you distort your face. You also distort your backgrounds, making them rough and unsettling extensions of your feelings.

VVG – That's what I see, a world of strange movements I'm reasonably sure aren't what you or most people see.

Paint it Blue

GTC – We see it in your work. That's why it resonates.

In late 1887 you seem to be fading from the world in *Self-Portrait with a Japanese Print* and another *Self-Portrait*.

VVG – No one really sees me, at least not as a person, more as a freak. And sometimes I understand that and want to be blurry and less visible to them as well as myself, and perhaps, for an instant, hurt a little less.

GTC – Your *Self-Portrait in Front of the Easel* is a masterpiece. You capture the torment we've discussed and also offer us a view of yourself at work. There's the canvas, much like those of the twenty-first century, and a pallet covered with different colors of paint, and you're holding several brushes. Thank goodness you aren't tempted by cameras and computers to stray from the basics.

VVG – I'd never use technology to make art. But I'd like to have it to study what I've painted.

GTC – Your *Self-Portrait from Arles* in September 1888 is dedicated to Paul Gauguin.

VVG – He doesn't understand my desire to help him and all other artists, to establish a community of painters, to nurture each other. As I look at my portrait I know he sees a man condemned.

GTC – Vincent, I think you must be experiencing some tranquility as you paint the *Self-Portrait* from November of that year. You don't look mellow but you do look almost comfortable.

VVG – Sometimes, in the mirror, with the right angle and lighting and a momentary lessening of pain, I come out less disturbed. Perhaps I was enjoying a flash of optimism about Gauguin living and painting with me.

GTC – You must again excuse my effusiveness when I tell you that here, from January 1889, is another masterpiece: *Self-Portrait with Bandaged Ear and Pipe*.

VVG – I prefer not to talk about my ear.

GTC – I don't want to, either. But you did paint it because you were driven to tell devastating truths. You're almost tranquil, at the same time, in *Self-Portrait with Bandaged Ear*.

VVG – A respite between storms.

GTC – Your *Self-Portrait from Saint-Rémy* in late August 1889 is another exceptional work. The scene behind you whirls and is as disturbing as the sky of *The Starry Night*. Your pallet is a shield.

VVG – My only protection.

GTC – Fortunately, you're quite disciplined. Your *Self-Portrait* from September 1889 features swirling blues and green on your jacket and behind you and even some on your face.

VVG – I'm being consumed.

GTC – I call this one the (Boxer) *Self-Portrait*. You look like a man who's taken some shots.

VVG – I have.

GTC – Why do you no longer paint yourself?

VVG – Land is less tormenting.

Vincent Talks to Patient

(This conversation occurred in a local mental health facility.)

Mental Patient – You don't know the trouble I've had.

Vincent van Gogh – I had quite a few problems, too.

MP – Not like mine. Your paintings generate hundreds of millions of dollars a year. And all the reproductions, merchandising, books, movies…you must've known you'd someday be rewarded. I'm homeless most of the time.

VVG – I had little gratification when I couldn't sell anything. I lived under quite modest circumstances.

MP – You always had a room and food and drink and plenty of art supplies. Paid for by your brother. My brother's in prison for life. I'm alone.

VVG – Loneliness was my eternal enemy.

MP – You lived with a woman and her child for a couple of years, didn't you?

VVG – An alcoholic prostitute with a noisy baby who were destroying my career. I escaped, but no woman had ever been interested nor would anyone again.

MP – No one's spent more than a paid night with me. I know I'm ugly.

VVG – No worse than I.

MP – You look all right in a few self-portraits. Some people must've been attracted.

VVG – They usually avoided me and spoke only to insult.

MP – People attack weakness. They know my mind's never been right. It's killing me. You're lucky they never gave you antipsychotic medications like I take. Sometimes they're worse than my illness.

VVG – I have a proposal. I'll sign over complete ownership of all my paintings if you'll trade places and let me have your medications.

MP – What if I can't stand the pain without them?

VVG – I'll also leave my gun.

Was Vincent Murdered

Two clever biographers appeared on *Sixty Minutes* and said Vincent van Gogh didn't really shoot himself in a wheat field more than a bumpy mile from town since he couldn't have walked so far bearing a wound destined to finish him in thirty hours.

Instead, the sleuthing biographers stated two teenagers in Auvers, a spot for swells outside Paris, had tormented Vincent, putting salt in his café drinks and, at the river, sending girlfriends over to taunt an already tormented man by pretending to offer love Vincent knew no one ever would.

The biographers therefore said they believe local gossip that one of the two punks shot Vincent, intentionally or not, in an Auvers building descending a half-mile to the inn where he staggered and a doctor noted the bullet was fired from a strange angle and a distance further than in most suicides and perhaps from a point Vincent couldn't have reached.

The biographers also noted it's quite strange Vincent replied, "I think so," when police asked if he'd tried to commit suicide, and, as a case clincher, requested no one else be charged. I don't know who really shot Vincent who yearned to die but am positive I'd love to time travel and pistol whip the bullies.

Vincent Sells

"Vincent."

He ignored me.

"Listen, I'm the world's preeminent art auctioneer, and I understand value."

"Nothing's more valuable than a gift to a friend."

"Give them books about yourself."

"I want to give them my work."

"You can. These books are beautifully illustrated."

"That's not the same."

"Then give them prints, reproductions. They're undetectable to most people."

"I want them to have originals."

"Impossible."

"They're mine."

"Not anymore. They've been sold, often several times each."

"I'm reclaiming them. Stand aside."

He picked up *Portrait of Dr. Gachet* and handed it to an astonished man in the front row.

"For God's sake, that's a hundred fifty-one million."

"Francs?"

"Dollars."

"My only sale was forty francs."

"But you've long been unimaginably popular."

"Madame," he said to a matron, "please come here. I'd like you to have *Portrait of Joseph Roulin.*"

"I can't accept this," she said.

"No, she can't."

"Yes, she can. Here Madame."

"That's a hundred twelve million, Vincent."

"Dollars?"

"Yes."

"All right, here we have *Irises* for this lovely little child. How old are you, dear?"

"Seven," she said.

"Vincent, you can't just give a painting worth a hundred ten million dollars to a child. Besides, the Getty Museum owns it, and, adjusted for inflation, that's what they paid."

"Too bad. They're thieves. I assure you no one ever paid me for *Irises*. And here, my final *Self-Portrait*. I'd shaved my beard. Glad I've grown it back."

"That's a hundred three million, Vincent."

"Okay, I'll take the cash."

"Minus our commission."

"How much is that?"

"For you, we'll lower it to ten percent."

"That's still more than ten million."

"A pittance."

"I'll sell it myself and give ninety-three million to charity and use to rest to set up beautiful studios in Paris and Auvers."

"Will that make you want to live, Vincent?"

"Only if I'm able to find more relief than at the asylum in Saint-Rémy."

"Don't worry, treatment is infinitely better now."

"By the way, I can't decide whether to put *Starry Night* in my living room or give it away."

"For God's sake, Vincent, that painting would be worth three hundred million today."

"Where is it?

"At the Museum of Modern Art in New York."

"Go get it."

"I can't."

"Very well, I'll fetch it."

Paint it Blue

Women

George Thomas Clark

Protecting Surrealist Women

"Security, stop that man," I shouted at startled employees assigned to guard the distinguished collection of paintings by surrealist women currently living at Los Angeles County Museum of Art.

They groped at an athletic young man sprinting by and, along with me, chased him as he ran directly to *Birthday*, a self-portrait by Dorothea Tanning. We formed a semicircle and crept forward but he scoffed at us, turned, and jumped right into the painting and kissed both of Tanning's delightful breasts, bared by an open blouse, and then gently put his hands on her beautiful but quite serious face. Tanning, animated at last, pushed him away, alarming the predatory bird clawing a strange four-legged creature in the foreground, and the bird flew at the man who dashed straight back through a series of open doors, slamming each until finally shutting the bird out. Tanning stroked driftwood alive at the rear of her skirt, reopened all surreal doors, and resumed her elegant pose.

From gasping art patrons we learned the rascal had scampered over to Tanning's *Family Portrait* and begun speaking to the impossibly large paterfamilias who stared down at the family table, "Take off the icy glasses, Grandpa, I can't see your eyes. If not for your grim visage I'd think you were dead. Perhaps I should pull that noose-like orange tie."

To the man's delicate blonde wife sitting obediently at the table, he said, "Madame, please don't sit there like the family dog, begging for a plate in the maid's hand. Come with me. There's a better way."

The young lady didn't move, doubtless as cowed by her oppressive husband as distrustful of the interloper, who next appeared, quite uninvited, in Leonora Carrington's *Self Portrait 1937-38*.

"Comely you assuredly are, Madam," he said, "but flirt with you I cannot because your wild hair portends, if you'll excuse this revelation, a thorough mental breakdown followed by electroshock therapy and wretched drugs that won't help you regain the love of Max Ernst, who, alas, will forever be committed to Dorothea Tanning . I hope you'll try to forgive them. Meanwhile, I suggest you banish that misshapen three-breasted horse and turn to enjoy the

70

magnificent white stallion statue, and at the same time remove its base like a saber through your head. Better still, dash through the open window and jump on that real living stallion and ride far away."

Security and I probed the painting, seeking a point of entry. We failed to find one but startled the intruder who ran through the window and, cowboy style, leaped over the flanks of the white horse, landing on its back, and away they galloped. Where would he go? Where did he go? We heard nothing and had to examine each painting. There he was, riding the merry-go-round toward illusory *Hollywood Success* by Dorr Bothwell. Never has there been so anguished an amusement horse as this grimacing green creature upon which rides, perilously on her knees, a hooded and body-suited actress balancing herself with an extended and gloved left hand and a right hand brandishing garish pink and purple flowers I suspect no director ever noticed.

Our presumptuous guest looked disheartened, bolted from Hollywood, and sought gratification at *The Tea Party* by Sylvia Fein. Had this man no decency? Surely he'd read the artist in 1943 was in a stressed and delicate state due to her husband fighting in the war. And now she was alone at the party, not merely in a corner by herself but the only one there except for a feral blue-eyed cat staring at her. The man also stared at her as she gazed into a toy cup held by her wedding-band left hand, and clutched a bloody toy animal in her right. The sky was displeased en route to anger, and the man disappeared, whether because of fear or courtesy I do not know.

George Thomas Clark

Paula Modersohn-Becker Speaks

I have never been so happy and free. I love living in Paris, far from my husband, Otto, who knows I yearn to be an independent woman and artist but won't accept I feel he's smothering me with complaints I've abandoned him and had even abandoned him when we lived together in the artist's colony of Worswede in northern Germany. I'm weary of his efforts to domesticate me. I'm disgusted by his and the others' isolation from the world of dynamic change in art. I'm outraged by their indifference to my work. Now I'm blossoming at age thirty in 1906 and writing Otto I'm not ready for children.

I want to create great art and have been dedicated since childhood when my father, a railroad official in Bremen, and my aristocratic mother paid for my drawing lessons. It pleased them to have a daughter who could entertain with sketches but they worried and rebuked me when I declared this would be a career. They agreed if I attended school to be a teacher they'd also finance my studies in the Society of Women Artists in Berlin for two years ending in 1898. I then began living and painting in Worswede where I soon despaired among people who dwelled in antiquity. Please let me escape, I wrote my parents, and they funded a stunning six months in Paris, the capital of the world glowing with works of Gauguin and Van Gogh and Cezanne and Matisse and endless opportunities to paint and grow.

I did have to go home, though. My parents were affluent, not wealthy. But where was home? I supposed it was back in Worswede with the widower Otto, and we married in 1901. Sometimes Otto defended me when I was dismissed by male artists who predominated – only three women painters lived in the colony – but increasingly he became an adversary and through a beard-shrouded mouth pelted me with pedantic opinions. I peered into his 1903 diary and read: "Paula hates all conventions, and she has now fallen for the mistake of making everything angular, ugly, bizarre and wooden. The colors are great – but the forms? The style! Hands like spoons, noses like conkers, mouth like gashes, faces like imbeciles. She's attempting too much... She won't listen to advice, as usual."

Paint it Blue

I wasn't going to paint the peasants and their world as a paradise without sickness or problems. I wasn't going to paint myself that way anymore, either. My 1902 *Self-Portrait with Trees in Blossom* creates a corona around my head that, for an instant, I almost liked. I more deeply examined myself in a 1903 *Self-Portrait* but still emerged too pretty and content. I changed that by escaping to Paris that spring. I hated asking Otto for the money and he bristled as he complied. That memory, in part, inspired another 1903 *Self-Portrait*, this one with a dark and foreboding background surrounding my pensive face.

Back to Worswede I inevitably came and stayed till I couldn't any longer and returned to Paris for two months in 1905 before going back to the dreary moors in northern Germany and telling Otto I wanted him no more. In February 1906 I forever escaped to Paris. Why would I ever leave? I'm painting like a whirlwind. My *Self-Portrait on her Sixth Wedding Day* shows me topless and relaxed and pregnant though I'm in no such physical state. My heart and mind are fertile. My life is aglow. I paint *Reclining Mother and Child* as a big, happy naked mother, brunette above and below, curling arms and legs around her infant.

Otto, I write, I shall never have a child with you. I'm becoming somebody. I am somebody. A week later I'm so lonely and insecure I write him, "My wish not to have a child by you was only for the moment...If you have not completely given up on me, then come here soon so that we can try to find one another again. The sudden shift in the way I feel will seem strange to you. Poor little creature that I am, I can't tell which path is the right one for me."

We are together in Paris and I get pregnant in February 1907. I feel it and sense Otto does too. We return to Worswede. I'm relieved to be a wife again and finally waiting for a baby. But in a letter I warn my sister "not to write me another postcard with words like 'diapers' or 'blessed event.'" I don't like sharing that with other people. I'm going to be a different kind of mother. In a November photograph I do, however, look quite traditional and serene sitting in a soft place and holding my newborn daughter's face close to mine. A few days later an embolism strikes and I'm gone at age thirty-one.

George Thomas Clark

Flowers of Séraphine Louis

Are you sure they've really made a movie about me? I can't imagine. I'm just from a family of farmers and laborers, and all day I'm either on my knees scrubbing floors with a brush or cooking meals or listening to fussy ladies tell me what else to do and how to do it. I know I'll never escape. I can't. No man wants me. I'm plain and plump and more than that I don't think I want a man because there are too many voices in my head and I'm usually more comfortable talking to trees before triple-locking the door to my dingy apartment.

I feel best when alone and no one can see blood from meat I've secretly collected in bottles or oil from church lamps or juices of fruits and vegetables. Oh, I also get some regular painting supplies from the local store when I can. But I don't like the storekeeper asking me questions. I don't even like him saying au revoir and don't reply since I don't want to see him again though I know I'll have to.

I don't feel right with anyone but my canvases on the floor. Over them I lean as I brush and caress colors alive with visions in my head. Some employers and others, who demand to see my early small works, laugh at me and say I'm wasting time. I fear they may be right until Wilhelm Uhde, a German art dealer with a gallery in Paris, visits Senlis in the pretty French countryside and rents a place my employer owns and that I clean, and accidently sees some of my flowers and says they're quite good, and he wants to help me but the Great War starts and he almost doesn't get out of France and has to leave his great collection.

I don't care about the war or anything else except painting which I do with passion that gets my feelings on canvas so I can see brilliant flowers crawling like caterpillars and shining like fresh fruit. Herr Uhde returns to Senlis in 1927 and says he thought I was dead but is thrilled with my improving work and right away begins to represent me and sells lots of my paintings, and I tell him to get me big canvases, two meters high, so I can fill them with images I have to express and that now earn me a grand monthly allowance.

People appreciate my work so much I know I'm going to be rich and don't need to wait to buy beautiful decorative items for my new large apartment that is grand but not grand enough as I decide I need

74

a mansion and prepare to buy it and more elegant clothes to replace the rags I've always worn and know I'm in heaven until some 1929 crash when Herr Uhde says he and his clients are broke and that I am too. How can I be broke? Just go out and sell some more of my paintings, I tell him. He claims he can't. I know why. He doesn't like my paintings anymore, and I curse him for destroying my wonderful new world. I refuse to return to the old one. I make a new one in my head and am taken away and locked up and don't remember much and what I do remember I want to forget but am thankful I don't have to paint anymore since it "has gone into the night."

Edgar Payne v. Elsie Palmer Payne

Edgar and Elsie Palmer Payne are arguing again. They've been arguing twenty years since marrying in 1912. I don't know why they got married but we shouldn't second guess people. They were young painters in love. They traveled the nation and world but Ozark Edgar retained backward views on women working.

Given my desperate domestic shortcomings, I'm unqualified to advise Edgar and Elsie and anyway have no right to do so. But I'm tired of yells from their home and studio as I nightly walk my dog in glorious Southern California. This time I step up and bang their door. Edgar answers, gnawing his pipe as if paid per tooth mark.

"Listen, Edgar, your mountains are pretty but always the same and you're simply not talented as Elsie," I say. "It's time for you to be a modern man and subordinate your career to hers. Unlike you, she can paint people and streets and rooms. She creates lives and feelings. She's an artist. You're a talented illustrator."

He slams the door but I block it with both palms and hear Elsie say, "He's right, Edgar. I forever pack and unpack, I cook, clean house, run errands, I bear the young, I do everything. I'm too tired to do what I must."

"That's your destiny as it has been women's throughout millennia."

"Not anymore. This is 1932, and this is Los Angeles. I shall have more time for my work."

"Not in my house."

"Perhaps this should now be my house."

"You'd be frightened and weak without me."

"I'd be an artist unchained."

"Very well, I'm weary of living with an unchained tiger. I'll move to Laguna Beach.

"Now, sir, get off my property."

I left. Two weeks later, so did Edgar, and Elsie blossomed.

Elsie's Bus Stop

Listen, I'm shapely and you may like my sexy eyes and want to kiss full black lips but don't think I'm on Sunset Boulevard waiting for you. I'm waiting for a bus to take me to a job few would choose and, as my arms extend hands in front of a sweet spot, I've got both eyes on everyone, especially you. Got to be careful on this cheap street. Might step in garbage or get bit by dogs. People worry me more. Thank God that mean looking old man behind is occupied with a pretty lady in green dress and matching green hat. She's with him so she can dress like that, and you know why he's with her. Don't forget, you'll never be with me. Wish I could dress my children like that mother down the street. Her little girl looks so cute in a short skirt and warm sweater. Good thing the mother's holding her hand. That man nearby looks like a weasel and could be trouble. Here's the bus just in time.

George Thomas Clark

Pollock Assists Lee Krasner

Some of you may disapprove but I mustn't care since I know what I've got to do to make *Polar Stampede* right. My abusive, alcoholic, bipolar, philandering, supremely-celebrated husband, Jackson Pollock, is five years dead in 1961 after he'd drunkenly, and I believe with suicidal determination, gunned his car through the night into a tree. I don't begrudge anyone the right to induce eternal relief, especially after lifelong agony, but Jackson surely should've taken his final ride alone and not with two young women, killing one while wounding his girlfriend.

Jackson can still make it up to me. After my two burly assistants dig up and open his coffin, I'm thankful he's well-preserved and handsome, despite being a bald corpse bludgeoned by glass and steel. My plan thus proceeds. Jackson is taken to my studio, and with a powerful compressor I pump blue and black and umber paint into his body and, most essentially, into his penis which, as planned, I'm able to expand into a manly three-foot implement for inspired application.

Unlike Jackson, whose most celebrated paintings were dripped onto canvasses on the floor, I tell my guys to hang a huge rectangular white canvas on the wall, and then place Jackson on his side about ten feet from the front center of the canvas. With considerable ardor, of an aesthetic nature, I clutch him first with my right hand about a foot from the top, then with my left a like distance from the bottom, and proceed to pump and squeeze with utmost vigor, and delight as thick trails of black and white and umber thrash the canvas and form islands of ever-moving color. With mad improvisation I proceed, firing paint up down right and left, wherever I need, whenever I want, and it's like Jackson's finally climaxing for me rather than himself, and celebrating that *Polar Stampede* will for centuries rouse people to stand back and realize I sometimes kick his ass, and do so with large splotches and thrusts, not the little drips of Jackson, and forever avoid being pigeonholed as little Lee Krasner, the abandoned and aesthetically-dependent wife of a wild man I must hastily cremate rather than risk using him in this manner again.

Lens of Diane Arbus

In the most fundamental sense I'm not photographing giants and midgets and the deformed and tattooed and transvestites and the normal my lens makes disturbed; I'm examining what I know myself to be: a misfit who's always hated that my parents are wealthy. I'm humiliated having nannies. I cringe at the deference of strangers. I'm embarrassed by lavish foreign vacations. I detest all my privileges. As an adult, I brood because I'm my husband's commercial photography assistant and not really a photographer. I have to escape. We separate in 1959 after eighteen years marriage. I'm thirty-six and have been taking some photography classes. I get commercial assignments but they depress me. I need subjects who compel me to proclaim: "I don't press the shutter. The image does."

On my own, with two daughters and without a trust fund, I discover my artistic self in photographs starting in the early 1960's. Tattooed *Jack Dracula* has raccoon eyes and wings on his forehead and chest and images all over. *The Backwards Man in his Hotel Room* features a head and torso facing one way and feet and legs pointing the other. The *Man from World War Zero and his Wife* bears three eyes and two noses his wife forgives. In 1962 *The Child with a Toy Hand Grenade* appears a lunatic ready to attack Central Park. All other photos that day make the child look normal. Those photos are forgotten.

Through my lens *A Castle at Disneyland* suggests the residence of Dracula. *The Human Pincushion* bears long pins through an eyebrow, his cheeks, lips, neck, chest, and arms. *Retired Man and his Wife at Home in a Nudist Camp one Morning* make you wish they were wearing clothes. Pretty young *Triplets in their Bedroom* look like they're waiting to be embalmed. A *Teenage Couple on Hudson Street* are objectively cute but in my frame somehow strange. *Russian Midget Friends in a Living Room on 100th Street* evoke Iron Curtain horrors as well as genetic disaster. *Jane with Son Ned* shows a mother with a head twice the size of her adult son's. The attractiveness of a *Puerto Rican Woman with a Beauty Mark* is overridden by her demonic gaze.

Some critics accuse me of degrading my subjects, making them "victims of my mocking lens." I disagree. My work is art, not satire. My art either illuminates what is there or could be there, lurking. My celebrated 1967 *Identical Twins* prompts their father decades later to tell *The Washington Post:* "We've always been baffled that she made them look ghostly. None of the other pictures we have of them looks anything like this."

How could they? I'm photographing a mind that is "literally scared of getting depressed. And it is so goddamn chemical, I'm convinced. Energy, some kind of special energy, just leaks out and I am left lacking the confidence to even cross the street."

When pain doesn't immobilize me I pick up my camera. In 1967 my *Patriotic Young Man with a Flag* resembles a halfwit. It's a matter of photographic selection: throw out the normal and showcase the bizarre. You can do it, too. You can find a *Seated Man in a Bra and Stocking* and high heels. You can capture a *Naked Man being a Woman.* You can locate a *Masked Man at a Ball* who may be the *Phantom of the Opera.* You can transform *A Family on their Lawn one Sunday in Westchester* into a scene from the *Twilight Zone.* You can immortalize an *Elderly Couple* before they die. You can shoot *A Dominatrix embracing her Client.* You can study *A Jewish Giant at Home with his Parents in the Bronx* and lament that the young man's head, even atop a curved and crippled spine, almost touches the ceiling far above his tiny parents. You can record smiling retarded people in *Untitled* photos from 1971. And, if necessary, you can swallow a handful of pills and slash your wrists.

Paint it Blue

The Human Canvas

Growing up "bourgeois" in 1940's Pasadena did not make Barbara T. Smith reserved, it made her ambitious. She wanted the boyfriend she had but her parents disapproved and sent her to study art at Pomona College where she could likely find an upstanding husband. Initially, she encountered profound depression that rendered her shaking at parties and unable to eat or sleep. She overcame social (if not emotional) difficulties by being "pretty," and soon obtained a suitable boyfriend, and future mate, and was pregnant before she graduated. Her lack of technical artistic skill wasn't an issue at the time: she had her first child and was depressed. She bore another and was more depressed. She entered therapy and improved, and gave birth to her third child, and started working at the Pasadena Art Museum and collecting art with her husband.

The marriage eventually disintegrated, however, and Smith realized she needed to go back to art school, in this case Chouinard Art Institute, to acquire technique she hadn't at Pomona. This shortcoming may have been due to inadequate curriculum, which she recently suggested, or lack of diligence. Really, Barbara T. Smith could paint well but didn't much want to. She wanted to make her body the medium. She either donned costumes or undressed, instructing viewers to behold and photographers to aim their cameras.

In 1968 Smith, the bourgeois homemaker, hosted "Ritual Meal," a dinner party where guests arrived in surgical attire and ate their meal with surgical implements while films of "open-heart surgery were projected on the walls around them. The experience gave the illusion of consuming a human body... Some of the guests had very strong physical reactions and were not able to eat meat for days afterwards."

Smith was just as bold for her 1977 "Pucker Painting," eagerly disrobing at an exhibition and exposing her no longer taut, but still attractive, mid-forties body. Her written instructions were:

"Choose a Color
Put it on your Lips
Kiss the 'Canvas'

81

So as to Make a Beautiful Painting"

Some art lovers demurred but eventually lots planted painted lips all around her belly button and on her arms and legs and face and on her lips.

"Did hundreds of people kiss you that day?" I asked.

"Unfortunately, only dozens did. Hundreds would've made a better painting."

Changes in Nude

when
i bought
her
naked
portrait
i thought
what a
bag
now i
worry
she's
too hot

George Thomas Clark

Kill the Whale

in upscale santa
monica gallery
painting covers high
long wall with
body of deceased
whale some call
leviathan being
chopped and sliced
before blubber
expertly pulled away
by crew of hot
females stuns like
old classical work
but with live
characters even
whale carcass

examine to learn
what mural painted
on but detect only
wall must be thin
canvas something
they can pull
down and remove
from room price
not on list says
to inquire and do
told ask karen
liebowitz who
painted *magical
thinking* fifteen
days for just this
time and space
mural to be
destroyed end
show but don't

Paint it Blue

worry can
hire to paint
this wherever
want

too much waste
in world can't
permit destruction
will hire same
joyous female
crew which doubtless
operates modern
machinery there on
moonless night to
demolish all gallery
except whaling wall
and truck to safe
house at gallery
will leave note
denouncing aesthetic
suicide

Romancing Women

My friend Higgins, the eternal bachelor, had been urging me to introduce him to some of the vibrant women in the current *Birth of Impressionism* show I curated at the de Young Museum in lush Golden Gate Park. All right, I ultimately told him last week, come on over, park in the new and convenient garage under the remodeled museum, and I'll introduce you to two ladies.

"Only two?"

"Don't be greedy."

Breathless and a tad sunburned, Higgins entered my office at the de Young and complained the vast garage was full, the entrance barred, and that he'd confronted endless lines of parked cars on both sides of every street in this pristine urban paradise, and had to hoof it a mile through salty winds.

"Be thankful for this opportunity," I said. "Here's a ticket. The ladies are expecting you."

"But the lines to the exhibition are long as those of the cars. I'd be waiting for hours."

"That's necessary since the ladies insist on meeting you when others are present. Oh, very well, I'll come with you."

Flashing my badge, I led Higgins past the line on the first floor and descended into the bunker where we circumvented hundreds of ravenous art lovers, and I advised my friend to relax and comport himself in a chivalrous manner.

"First, I shall introduce you to the *Woman with Fans* by Edouard Manet in 1873. Her name is Nina de Cullias. She's a writer and poet and a sensational host of parties for the rich and talented. I needn't elaborate on her charm."

"Indeed, I've heard about her."

Attired in a long and elegant black dress and reclining in bed, her head supported by her left hand and the corresponding elbow planted in two plush pillows, she's backed by a wall displaying numerous colorful fans, and her seductive face is serene and confident.

"Maria, my dear, this is my friend Higgins," I said.

"Madame, I adore the way your silken black hair is styled up on your head and reveals your delightful cheeks and neck."

Maria de Cullias smiled at Higgins. She doubtless smiles at many men.

"I must tell you, Maria – if I may use your first name – that nothing on earth would delight me so much as exploring your lovely black dress."

While continuing to prop her head with left hand, she reached with her right hand across her body, under the pillows, retrieved a flask, and fired it at Higgins, nailing him in the forehead. She then pushed her face into the pillows and cried. I pulled my friend away.

"Are you a fool?" I said.

"Not at all. Everyone in Parisian high society is talking about her sexual appetites, which are fueled by alcohol."

"And I would hope your research revealed she's also frequently depressed. At any rate, your approach was impudent. Behave yourself over here."

We moved to *Haymaking*, an 1877 offering by Jules Bastien-Lepage, and beheld an exhausted and partially spread-legged woman, of peasant stock, who's sitting in a farm field and wearing a sack-like skirt, a cheap white blouse, and gray stockings that match her vest. Her look of sexual expenditure leaves her emotionally naked, an impression buttressed by the red-bearded man, hat covering his face, stretched out and asleep after haymaking her. This painting provoked a scandal when first exhibited.

"My dear," said Higgins, "I so enjoy farm work that I hope you'll let me join you tomorrow."

"My husband and I'd be delighted, sir," she replied.

"The gentleman is clearly tuckered out and incapable of satisfying you. I believe we should work alone."

The woman looked confusedly at Higgins before her face hardened.

"That man is a serf," Higgins continued. "A lady of your passion deserves a gentleman."

She bounded up and toward a point just off canvas, presumably to grab a pitchfork, and I pulled Higgins away.

"I'm ashamed of you," I told him.

"I merely responded to what these women so clearly desire."

"They don't desire it with a man who disrespects them. That's all for you, thank goodness."

"Please," Higgins said. "Introduce me to just one more."

"Very well," I conceded. "Follow me."

Shrouded in a deathly black dress and looking straight ahead in sagging profile, lifeless and unwashed gray hair plastered under a faded off-white bonnet, *Whistler's Mother* No. 1 sits stoically before us.

"Mrs. Whistler," I said, "please say hello to my friend Higgins, who wishes to dine with you this evening."

She turned toward us, examined Higgins, and smiled open a mouth of gray and probably false teeth before saying, "I should be delighted."

Expressionism

Expressionists Rouse L.A.

Driving the wine country route northeast from Ensenada up to Tecate out in the desert and waiting a half hour to be examined at the border before continuing north through more arid territory until hitting early but heavy Friday afternoon L.A. traffic had tired body and mind and burned seven hours when I pulled into the parking lot underneath the Los Angeles County Museum of Art. A sign said Lot Full but I declared no way, a car's coming out now, and the ticket machine agreed, raising the barrier. I needed a rush so was lucky to find a spot right away, hurried to the elevator, walked to a window, paid twenty-five bucks, bought a ticket and walked into the featured exhibit: *Expressionism in Germany and France: From Van Gogh to Kandinsky*.

"Get over here and give us a hand," said one of seven strong shirtless men pulling seven ropes attached to a board connected to four more the men hoist up and then let smash into baked brown dirt in a hole on a construction site. Standing proudly to the side of *The Pile Drivers*, painter Maximilien Luce swept his hand into the scene and said, "Go ahead."

"Sorry, but they've discarded their shovels and I want no part of hardpan nor do I care to inhale all that poison fuming out of smokestacks on the other side of the river."

"You're rather prim."

"The air's filthy even in 1902. Why don't you help the men you created?"

"Ordinarily I would, and many times have, but today I must greet patrons of this prestigious museum."

I'd taken three steps away when a man called, "We're *Sand Diggers on the Tiber* and the sand's hot and hideous and we're sick of it and the glare that burns and distorts everything, and we want out. Please, help us."

"Can't you do something?" I ask painter Erich Heckel.

"I didn't put them there. That's where they were when I arrived."

"What about that poor *Girl with Doll*. She's no more than ten. Do you claim she was naked when you arrived?"

"No, but she's willing to display herself and her doll for art."

Paint it Blue

"You're skirting pedophilia, Heckel. You mustn't paint children in a sexual manner. It's indecent. For goodness sakes, clothe the girl and undress her doll."

Around I turn and spot a gaunt young man and say, "Ernst Ludwig Kirschner, this is a pleasure."

"Oh, why is that?"

"I suppose it's the profound edginess in your work. Look at this frightening but sexy green lady, enflamed by red hair and lips, in *Reclining Nude in Front of Mirror*.

"What's in that long pipe, ma'am? Getting a little loaded, are we?"

"Come here," she says. I comply, and she blows smoke in my face. Granted, I'd like to have done her but no way do I want the morose *Woman in Green Blouse* who's studying me like an indolent shark I won't let catch me, dashing to *Dodo with a Big Feather Hat*. I like her big-nose pouty-red mouth left profile. I know she wants it. She's been waiting, full body under black dress.

"Good afternoon," I say.

She doesn't speak. She doesn't move. I look to Kirchner for assistance but he's stretched on the blanket next to the reclining nude, smoking her pipe.

Very well, Kirchner, I won't interrupt. I'll walk over to your masterwork, *Street, Berlin*. It's 1913 and for these wealthy and insolent creatures there are no problems. They're overdressed and painted up and prancing on a pink sidewalk just before World War One which will sicken if not kill them, and the aftermath will be worse. Nazism will consume them and Kirchner, too, calling him degenerate and rejoicing when he crumbles.

"Might as well keep smoking, Ernst. Smoke all night long."

I need something strong but not that. "Say, Max Pechstein, please introduce me to *Magdalena: Still Life with Nude*. I won't temporize. I love her long black hair. I crave her full breasts. I yearn for her thighs."

"Indeed," says Pechstein. "I've just finished entertaining her and am preparing to return."

"Fine idea," I say, and ease over to *Still Life with Nude, Tile, and Fruit*. Surely Pechstein can't delight both at once. This dark sensuous woman has just emerged from a bath and is peering around a blanket to see who's there. I am. I'm here for ripe lips and black hair and will devour the fruit between us.

A good while later I pass Emil Nolde who says, "I'm a bit lonely."

"That's a fine *Ship in Dock*, but not as alluring as a lady, particularly since it's a rough night and the ship's been battered by the sea that batters itself and the sky is the sea."

To a brighter place I step in the crowded museum gallery and say, "Good afternoon, Paula Modersohn-Becker. It's a delight to meet you and, as ever, a pleasure to view your work. I adore *Seated Nude Girl with Flower Vases* and know that you, unlike some of your libidinous male colleagues, are an adoring mother."

"You're most gracious.

I bow, hoping she saw the photograph of herself with baby days before the embolism. A tragedy, she was only thirty-one.

I spin and walk head down to a wall offering *Reflective Woman* by Karl Schmidt-Rottluff. She's sitting nude beneath a green blanket that bares her shoulder and arms. Her left hand may have just wiped away a tear. She ignores me and everyone else. She must know she'll soon have to enter a world like Schmidt-Rottluff's *Garden Street Early in the Morning*. The street isn't really a street but a chaotic corridor red, pink, green, orange, and blue. I'm not walking there and neither should you.

Better to visit voluptuous *Modjeko, Soprano Singer*, striking in a red, green, and white feathery hat and low-cut white dress, as she entertains at the circus and in halls of burlesque.

The instant she finishes this song, I ask, "Ma'am, might we dine after your performance?"

With a large hand she lifts her feathery crown and says, "I'm a man, fool, but if you still want, come by."

Backing away I motion for painter Kees van Dongen. "What's the deal, sir, shouldn't you post a warning sign?"

"Relax," he says, "go get the girlfriend on the right."

That lucky man in *Girlfriends* hugs his naked woman who's so hot for him. "I'll take her," I tell van Dongen. "Please, distract her boyfriend."

"Look more closely on the left, and note the title ends with s."

Heinrich Campendonk waves to come over and says, "You're

taking matters literally. Here, enter a world with some abstract elements in *Harlequin and Colombine*."

In a beautiful multi-colored scene of undefined elements I must filter to find the skeletal man with sharp hands on the left. He's looking at or over a giant red rodent who's malevolently looking at a single-breasted female with open thighs behind a strange dog-like creature who's not her guardian.

"Good day," I tell Herr Campendonk.

I want something real and dependable and of my world. Thank goodness, there's Vincent. That is him, isn't it? Oh dear, he's romanticized himself in his self-portraits. I must try to help.

"Vincent, how do you do? Ordinarily I'd be speechless in the presence of genius, and of such celebrity, but I'm soothed by your pretty, almost Thomas-Kinkade-like *Restaurant of the Siren at Asnieres*. This must be your most tranquil scene."

"It's from 1887 and, for perhaps an hour, I felt like a human being people would like."

"People do like you, Vincent. They love you."

"They're appalled, like you. Don't deny it. Step over here, to *Wheatfield with Reaper* and remember I painted it two years later, after self-mutilation and while hospitalized at Saint-Remy. Imagine working in a field burned by morbid sun into fiery wheat undulating like snakes, ready to engulf. Here, look at *The Poplars at Saint-Remy*. These two sinuous trees knife a malicious blue sky and white lighting in my head. Go away. I can't stand how your stare."

"Over here," says Paul Gauguin, patting my shoulder. "I lived with that man and almost died by his hand. But I escaped. And you can too. Here are *Haystacks in Brittany*, lush and inviting in a calm green pasture under a placid blue sky. Go on over behind the haystack on the left and get undressed. I'll send the farm girl and mind her cows."

I pity Vincent living with Gauguin whose young woman in white bonnet and long dress smells like hay and slaps like a boxer.

"The hell with women," I tell Henri Matisse. "I just need some energy from *Still Life with Oranges*."

"Eat all you want."

I take only three on the table and leave undisturbed those in the elevated white dish. As Matisse scans the gallery I ease to *Nude Study in Blue.* Standing and covering herself with joined hands, she's graceful and sexy but I hope also a little shy. I move back to the still life, grab two oranges, and return to the lady standing in a stark room. I don't knock. I don't ask. I walk in.

Twentieth Century Revealed

In 1899 my wife and three children and assorted siblings and in-laws encircled my bed and held my hand and told me I'd been a good man who would forever be at peace in heaven where they would soon join me. I did not believe that, though I declined to debate the point. Often enough they'd listened with chagrin as I characterized all things divine as myths. I must have been correct. Never did I see anyone after I closed my eyes. Why I have suddenly been plucked from the abyss and permitted to walk and feel again, I do not know. And I haven't time to speculate. I have but five minutes and the assignment to examine two specific paintings in the Los Angeles County Museum of Art. Then on that basis, and no other, I will be called back to assess the Twentieth Century.

In the Expressionism gallery the first work, by Ludwig Meidner, is titled *Apocalyptic Landscape 1913*. Jagged clouds black and white rip the sky and menace the earth where people clad in funereal black flee in all directions on streets that split below, preparing to devour them. In the background large buildings buckle and moan. Now I feel those black clouds like giant birds hovering to strike.

In the same gallery I am pulled across the room to *The Orator*, a 1920 painting by Magnus Zeller. At once I note a less-wry Zeller could have titled it *The Demagogue*. On stage the great speaker stands, mouth open toward the heavens, his arms extended also high, hands open in supplication and fingers extended like knives. Around the stage crazed listeners consume the leader with cavernous eyes and pant he's the only one who can save them. And he is not merely a man's man. The only child in this painting is duly enraptured, and the singular lady is gasping and doubtless ready to rip her nude dress and give everything to the leader. She's chosen a good year, 1920, when that young man starts ranting in Bavaria.

Very well. I'm home in my box, and need remark no further about any century.

George Thomas Clark

Ernst Ludwig Kirschner

I don't like to fight but have to since my head makes me attack Van Gogh's work as "nervous and tattered" which I am in 1906 painting my lover in *Woman's Head with Sunflowers* using brushstrokes wicked orange and yellow and deadly blue down three sunflowers onto her downcast face she rebukes me for making her look so bad and calls me a Van Gogh disciple which I reject.

I'm an innovator I will be soon in 1912 in the *Red Elizabeth Bank* showing Berlin buckling under purple-sky winter swelter in a world without people save two walking cadavers in the right foreground. Berlin knows it's that way and belts me again in crumpling gray *Nollendorf Square* where four trains converge.

In 1914 I'm happy to join the army and fight in the glorious Great War and am so attuned to what's happening in 1915 I go mad not really mad I just crumple and have to be treated for my nervous and tattered condition that takes me away from the Great War and allows me to paint *Self-Portrait as a Soldier* with dead eyes and a killer face above an amputated right painting hand that's not really gone it's fine it's leading modern art into the age of expressionism. Today you'd need tens of millions to buy my 1915 *Street Scene in Berlin* with elegant and sexy human monsters gliding down an eerie street.

I don't like the city I don't like Germany in 1918 I move to the Swiss mountains with my third wife Erna. From the city they howl Kirchner you need your painterly friends and patrons but I don't need them I need solitude because I'm rather tense knowing enemies are planning to get me. I won't let them I'm too good I pre-date many of my paintings and stress I'm the leader and everyone's copying me. In 1933 the Nazis call me a degenerate artist and strip me of membership in the Berlin Academy of Arts in a country I haven't visited in years but in 1937 the Nazis still sting when they confiscate six hundred of my works from museums and sell and burn many but don't get all and they don't get me in 1938 I get myself.

Otto Dix in The Trench

I'm amazed people in trenches reported I was calm before battle, seated by myself sketching images and impressions of the Great War, and then roused on command to fire my machinegun and slaughter scores or more of the enemy until hostilities waned and I quietly sat back down and relaxed as I resumed sketching. I sketched so I wouldn't scream, putting feelings on papers I reviewed a few years later when painting *The Trench* in which ghosts and a gas-masked soldier lurk amid heads, limbs, and rubble choked by dust and colored by sky gray as death.

Who could relax being several times wounded, once by shrapnel in the neck that almost killed me before they stopped the bleeding? Sometimes I tried to ease up by going to whorehouses. That helped briefly before I began, every time I dropped my pants, to see women like one I portrayed in *Nude (for Francisco Goya)*. She's wicked as war, her hairy head an explosion, her mouth dangerous as a hyena's, her right hand a claw, and her feminine spot, for which we'd yearned and paid, a frightening hole covered by wild and filthy hair.

There was war even after the war and I had many nightmares, especially about crawling through destroyed houses, but should also be grateful. People often remarked I was the most masculine man in the room. And I met an art-collecting Dusseldorf doctor whose wife, Martha Koch, loved me as I adored her, and, as the doctor had already begun loving her older sister, we sustained our friendship and soon I had *The Artist's Family*, a wholesome and sexy wife and two beautiful children. I didn't do many portraits like that. Instead I did fifty etchings of *War* that show *Tangled Barbed Wire before the Trench* and *Battle Weary Troops Retreating* and a *Dead Man in the Mud* and a *Bomb Crater with Flowers* and more. In my large triptych *Metropolis* I offer a legless veteran on the left leered at by a hungry dog and ravenous whore, and gaudily dressed wealthy women strutting like whores by another maimed and indigent man on the right, and between them the garish bourgeoisie, clad in pink, yellow, and orange, dancing to a jazz band.

In this Germany we got Adolf Hitler in 1933, and his Nazis promptly ousted me from my position as an art professor, and I responded with *The Seven Deadly Sins* – old witch Avarice is bent over

97

George Thomas Clark

squeezing money while Envy rides her back and skeletal Sloth, like a Nazi, wields a scythe, and Lust craves some of that power sucking the tit she squeezes with her right hand, and Anger waits to move in with his horns while ears-plugged, anus-mouth Pride points his coarse Hitler-nostrils like a gun into the sky, and Gluttony helmets his foolish head with a cooking pot.

I wasn't surprised the Nazis put some of my expressionistic paintings in their exhibition of Degenerate Art in 1937 and later burned them and some others from museums. I'd liked to have machine-gunned the bastards or at least gotten away but couldn't emigrate because they would've "confiscated (my) stable full of paintings here." During World War Two I restrained myself, and protected my family, by painting landscapes that merely allude to illness around us. The Nazis still considered me an enemy and near the end forced me into the Volkssturm, that pitiful collection of aging men and naïve boys who marched into meat grinders at the front. I was captured by French troops and later painted *Self-Portrait as a Prisoner of War* that reveals me gray-bearded and battered but stoic. And when I got home I happily retrieved *The Seven Deadly Sins* and brushed a weird little mustache onto the face of Envy.

Paint it Blue

Nazis Attack Karl Schmitt-Rottluff

My god, I thought I was rid of the Nazis after World War II. For years they'd been calling my paintings perverse and defective, and in 1937 Adolf Ziegler, the man Hitler named President of the National Chamber of Fine Arts and thus arbiter of everything that could and could not exist in the aesthetic world of National Socialism, wrote me a horrific letter declaring more than six hundred of my paintings "had to be seized" from German museums, and many were displayed without frames in dark rooms, along with the works of Ernst-Ludwig Kirschner, Otto Dix, and other notables, in the Nazi exhibit of Degenerate Art. Ziegler further upbraided me for not contributing to the "advancement of German culture" and continuing to be unreliable and therefore unworthy of being involved in "any activity – professional or amateur – in the field of graphic arts."

This decree would naturally have been devastating from anyone but was particularly obscene from Adolf Ziegler who painted insipid young ladies and was known among creative artists as the "master of German pubic hair." His authority and popularity perished with Hitler in 1945, and thereafter he was shunned by art galleries and institutions until his death in 1959. By contrast, I received awards and many retrospectives in museums and in 1976 died a renowned artist.

I make the forgoing statement not to boast but ask why the hell Adolf Ziegler is now trying to rip my painting – *Autumn Landscape in Oldenburg, 1907* – from the wall of the distinguished Thyssen-Bornemisza Museum in Madrid? With neither hesitation nor sympathy I from behind seize Ziegler around the neck and choke him into dizziness before letting him drop. I cock my leg to kick him but instead demand, "Explain yourself."

"Your expressionism still doesn't portray a happy, healthy, and racially pure vision of our Aryan paradise," he says. "This landscape is as unsettling as your portraits. Look at that morose blue barn roof threatening collapse and the dirty orange roof also about to buckle. They lack beauty and order, and so do the ominous green trees between them. Nature is magnificent, not malignant. And then, your fields are not pure green but threatened by red fire that can only disturb viewers. And in the foreground those dirty orange haystacks are simmering and troublesome rather than bountiful and serene."

"Ziegler," I say, "those familiar with your earliest adult work said you were also a modernist painter, albeit one of limited skill."

"I did no such work. Show me some."

"I suspect you destroyed it when you decided to become a Nazi."

"I painted what I was inspired to paint

"And you suppressed what inspired others."

"That's the eternal duty of fascists."

Degenerate Art

I assigned my art jury to pick the very best Germanic paintings for the spectacular House of German Art in Munich. When the process of selection was well underway, I stopped by to see. Most of the chosen paintings were fine. But some were not.

"This one," I said. "You can't possibly think this one is good. What's it doing here? This is garbage. That's right, don't answer. Are you idiots? This is manure plastered on canvas. It shouldn't be here. It certainly won't be in the exhibition. And that one, over there. Yes, that one. Stand aside. That's worse. It looks worse the closer I get. I made my standards clear. What's this garbage doing here? And over there. That's right. There. Get the hell out of my way. Don't try to stand in front of it. Move. This is horrible, too. I can't stand this. You must be idiots. I told you what I wanted, what the House of German Art had to have. Oh, shit. And over there, too. There's another one. Move. Move."

Grabbing the perverted expression of the human soul, a hand on each side of the frame near the top, I grunted and lunged and kicked my right boot hard right through the canvas and yanked back, ripping even more. I flung that frame down, breaking it, and stomped to another bad painting, the jury clearing wide in my wake, and grabbed that one and jack-booted it, too, and threw it down hard and stormed around and kicked everything obscene.

By July 1937 my requirements had been realized, and people all over Munich celebrated the great opening of the House of German Art. On the walls hung several hundred of the purest expressions of healthy creativity. In my revolutionary speech I said: "We're creating a new human type, a strong joyful healthy creature, and I can't tolerate depictions of malformed cretins and cripples that bespeak a highly defective vision. If the cultural Neanderthals responsible for such abominations don't desist, then I'll certainly have them hospitalized if they're crazy, or jerked into jail if the criminal acts are intentional."

While Germans enjoyed this opportunity to see the best in art, I provided an enlightening contrast, the *Exhibition of Degenerate Art*, also in Munich. Thousands of perverse paintings, by lunatics like

101

Kirchner, Kandinsky, and Chagall, had been purged from our museums, and several hundred of the worst comprised a display so appalling that I ordered it taken around Germany. Almost three million paid to see what degeneracy really was, and many wrote urging us to tie up the artists next to their paintings so everyone could spit in their faces.

Africa and America

George Thomas Clark

Look at William H. Johnson

I'm standing near the first Self-Portrait William H. Johnson paints and am about to speak to him when a female student marches up and says, "We're going on a picnic tomorrow, William. Please join us."

"Thank you, but I haven't time."

"There's a dance this weekend. Why don't you come with me?"

"I'm afraid I cannot."

"Why not?"

"I will be painting. I will be reading. I…"

"You're a very handsome young man, William. I wish you'd join us once in a while."

"You're most kind, but I simply cannot."

"I hope you don't mind my asking, but are you part Negro or Mexican or Arab?"

"I am a Negro. Now, Miss, please excuse me."

I move to another work from his 1923-26 days at the National Academy of Art in New York. This painting is called Portrait of a Woman, one of four he so titles as a student. She's a tired and tough looking woman, red ribbon in her hair and a worn black bra above her bare stomach, and it looks like she may have just finished entertaining someone.

"William, please excuse me, but I must tell you I hope you aren't a client of that woman."

"I beg your pardon?"

"You must understand the dangers."

"What dangers? I'm an artist."

"You are, indeed, and growing all the time. In France your work changes. Here are two excellent examples from the late twenties when you start to paint what your mind sees: those unsteady Houses on a Hill appear ready to slide down the mountain and the Village Houses, Cagnes-sur Mer sway forward and swallow sky over a buckling street where two people shouldn't be."

"Who are you?"

"An independent admirer of the arts. By the way, I met your girlfriend, Holcha Krake, several years ago in Denmark. She's a delightful lady, bright, witty, outgoing." I don't mention some busybodies are surprised a robust man of twenty-nine takes up with a lady of forty-five.

"I miss her when I return to New York, but I must sell some paintings here and visit my family in Florence, South Carolina."

"I'm sure your trip is personally gratifying and an artistic success. I like this portrait of your teenage brother, Jim, who appears bright, introspective, sad-eyed, and somewhat bemused by what his big brother's stroking on the canvas."

"Let's take a look at Jacobia Hotel," Johnson says. "Some critics contend it, and other works, are unduly influenced by Van Gogh and Soutine and French moderns. What do you think?"

"Everyone has influences whether or not he acknowledges them or is even aware. Jacobia Hotel is distinctly yours, and I believe its dilapidation is not only visually striking but a metaphor for the crumbling South. I must again tell you, William, that after painting this place I trust you didn't partake of anything dangerous."

"This crumbling hotel is now a flophouse, not a cathouse, and I resent your intrusive comments."

"It's quite unlike me to even broach such matters. Let's go back to Europe. Congratulations on your marriage to Holcha. It's wonderful many in Keterminde are impressed by your fast-improving Dutch as well as unique ways of painting the local people."

"A new verbal language is a companion to my new visual idiom."

"And quite powerful it is," I say. "I doubt the fisherman Old Salt, Denmark, sees himself in quite this way."

"We've already learned not to expect a photograph from Billy," says Old Salt. "I don't look this bad in person. My nose isn't so large and red, my face not quite that burned and weather-beaten, my eyes aren't so distant and unfriendly. But I'm crusty all right, and that's what Billy's got on this canvas."

"I hope your work is finding an audience in Denmark and elsewhere in Europe."

"I make some sales personally and also recently had my first show in Copenhagen. Now I have one in Oslo."

"This Self-Portrait of 1935 is quite novel. Your skin tones match the door and, between that small rumpled hat and an orange collar and red handkerchief, you look like a bearded swinger with edge."

"I'm no swinger but I always have an edge cutting inside."

"I hear you meet Paul Robeson and Edvard Munch. Your impressions?"

"Robeson's much more gregarious than I'll ever be, and Munch makes me seem like Robeson. Maybe I'm more like Munch, though. I can't picture Robeson spending a few years in rural Norway."

"There's a huge and overpowering work from that period."

"Midnight Sun, Lofoten. It brings more charges of being influenced by Van Gogh."

"Preposterous. Van Gogh's brightest sun is merely the moon of The Starry Night while your sun is a supernova heating the sky yellow and orange over barren blue mountains touched by snow and vegetation."

"I'm writing letters to the Harmon Foundation in New York, telling them my work belongs in major museums. Here's another: Self-Portrait with a Pipe. I stare at a threatening world, inhaling soot from my pipe and holding a small but sharp brush between myself and everyone else. Europe was so tranquil but now the Nazis are taking over and we know war's coming. Holcha and I leave in 1938."

"A wise move."

"Particularly in art, and frankly far beyond what I imagine. Every day I'm stimulated by the vibrancy of Negroes who enable me to feel and envision our history and our present. Many of them consider me reserved and serious but I think they enjoy my work. I paint naked black women, brown women, fat women, slender women, big-busted women standing, sitting, reclining, and laying on their sides, all sexy women beautiful in unique ways. I paint Joe Louis lambasting another white man. I paint cool couples dressed in stylish hot clothes in cafes and on the streets of Harlem. I paint street musicians guitar-picking and fiddling. I paint a blind singer. I paint acrobatic couples doing the jitterbug. I paint a sleepy-eyed father, mother and child ready for Early Morning Work. I paint farmers plowing, planting, digging, pumping water, and guiding horse-pulled wagons. I paint men, women, and children picking cotton and stuffing it into sacks. I paint exhausted workers during Lunchtime Rest. I paint worried but unbroken families and couples dealing with broken-down vehicles and mobile homes. I paint well-dressed parents Going to Church with their two boys in a wagon pulled by a blue-eared horse. I paint dignified congregants watching as the preacher, right arm in the heavens and left around a lady, proclaims, I Baptize Thee. I paint people in primitive but profound ways. I know Lincoln at Gettysburg III understands my language. His eyes are blazing blue as he stands before blue-eyed brown followers at the memorial to death.

"I don't get my first significant solo show in the United States until 1941, and I'm already forty. It's at a fine gallery. There are some sales and insightful reviews received but I can't make a living painting. I try not to become hysterical too often. Don't know what's causing that but it upsets Holcha, and I understand others have suffered more. A couple of years ago my brother-in-law died after the Nazis tortured him for being unique.

"And now the Japanese attack Pearl Harbor, compelling me to redirect my brush. Negro soldiers, smiling grimly, raise their right hands at the Induction Center. Negro soldiers train hard, marching Ten Miles to J Camp. Negro soldiers hang listless heads after the drudgery of K.P. Negro soldiers march in time to their morning bath. Negro soldiers skillfully operate artillery and gas masks as well as rifles with bayonets. Wounded Negro soldiers wait to be moved at Station Stop Red Cross Ambulance. The Operating Room awaits Negro soldiers. Negro nurses at the Knitting Party recover from helping their shattered men. Orange Moon Over Harlem examines victims of a race riot some of whom have gotten drunk and victimized themselves."

"I never see any portraits of Holcha. Have you painted her?" I ask.

"Thank God I haven't or it would kill me to look. She has breast cancer and soon is too weak to rise from her bed. By December 1943 she's in a filthy hospital. Some friends help us get her moved to a better place in January but I'm not there when she exclaims, 'I spent my happiest days in Norway with Billy.'

"'She's about to die,' the nurses tell a visiting friend.

"He calls and says, 'Get here quickly.'

"I do but Holcha's gone when I arrive. The following day I clutch her funerary urn.

"Maybe God will help. Maybe I'm the brown Christ, prayed for by beautiful brown women in Mount Calvary and Lamentation (Descent from the Cross). I really don't feel much better. Some exhibitions and meager sales don't help, either. In June 1944 I visit my family in Florence, South Carolina, only my second time there in a quarter century. Mom's still alive. Dad's more than a decade dead. My brothers and sisters are grown, and to one of their children, who won't open the door to a stranger, I say, 'Boy, I'm your uncle.'"

"Do they appreciate your art?" I ask.

"I damn well demand it. I turn the back porch into a studio and order everyone to be careful. I'm painting a Little Girl in Orange and a Little Girl in Green and my niece Li'l Sis and a barefoot Woman Ironing and my very dark Mom Alice and a light mother in Mom and Dad, the dad on the wall's far lighter than Mom's husband ever was.

"My money's running out. I've got to get back to New York to work in a navy shipyard. Imagine a man of my intellect and talent in his forties grinding away days in the most menial ways. I soothe myself thinking about Holcha. Maybe this also tortures me but memories are involuntary.

"In 1945 I begin my best and most ambitious works: the Fighters for Freedom series. I paint George Washington Signing the Declaration of Independence, accompanied by other serious white people. In Let my People be Free I paint Abraham Lincoln on the left and Frederick Douglass on the right and symbolic people hanging in the center. I paint Haile Selassie on a white horse, surrounded by sincere and somber people. I paint A Historical Scene with Mary McLeod Bethune surrounded by serious scholars. I paint Historical Scene – WWII showing happy world leaders and generals backed by planes and tanks and artillery. I'm starting to feel good again and know I can take these and similar works to Europe for a triumphant tour.

"'What the hell do you mean, they're disparate postage-stamp chatracters? Are you fools?' I ask formerly-supportive artists and collectors in New York. If I weren't a gentleman, I'd thrash them. I know Holcha loves these works and also understands in March 1946 when I write her mother and state my hope that sister Erna 'can take Holcha's place in this great journey.' I'm writing every person and foundation I can think of, demanding they return all my paintings. I must take all of Holcha's work as well as her ashes and clothes and spices and many other treasures."

"Isn't that too much?" I ask.

"No, I'll need everything for my new life. On a cold October day in New York I sail. Back in Denmark I'm so happy to see Holcha's family, which is my family too. They must quit asking me for Holcha's ashes, though. Every day I explain I have to keep something of my wife because her memory is always inside, urging me to endure."

"Why not give them the ashes," I say.

"I finally do and hope that'll help, and in December nervously travel to Copenhagen for my most vital moment since I long ago proposed to Holcha. Erna's small apartment is cramped by her daughter, son-in-law, and granddaughter staying there. My belongings fill the living room where I sleep several nights before saying, 'Musse, I must speak to you privately. We're artists and both still grieving for our lost husband and wife, who shared our creative journeys. Your desire must surely be great as mine. I know you'll want to join my European tour and take at least part of Holcha's place. You're the only one who ever could.'

"'Billy, that's the most insulting thing I've ever heard. I'm sorry, but you can't sleep here anymore. You can eat with us, but that's all. Good night.'

"Stung by a woman who could have rescued me, I gather my bags of art and clothes and enter a frigid Copenhagen night that bothers me not at all. Sometimes I sleep in dumps, others in the streets. I don't care. Every evening for dinner I return to Erna's and say, 'Musse, please let me know if you change your mind.' I think she will. It doesn't matter I'm getting dirty. When police arrest me for vagrancy, I reach into my coat pocket and wave six grand in their faces.

"'Where'd you get that?' says one officer.

"'I'm a renowned painter.'

"In March 1947 I arrange an exhibition in one of Copenhagen's finest galleries but Musse won't come and there aren't many sales. People here don't understand my newest work. Soon I take a ferry to Oslo and want other passengers to quit staring. 'Here's a pretty picture for you,' I say, pouring a bottle of red soda onto the white tablecloth.

"In Oslo I live outside, hauling my things around the city."

"Wouldn't a shower and warm place to sleep be nice?" I suggest.

"Perhaps I do need better quarters and start to sleep in a shed on the wharf. Two policeman come and one says, "Put your money away and come with us."

"They watch me closely in a cell and later that night take me to the hospital. Several days later a doctor tells me I'm suffering from 'advanced syphilis-induced paresis.' What the hell's that? In November they send me and my paintings back to the United States. At first I'm unhappy being in a mental hospital. Then I don't really believe I'm here. I'm somewhere else."

Charles White Endures

1. Goodbye Father

daddy's dead but
momma says we've got
to sit way back in church
and from there
i watch everyone
especially the family
in front
crying even harder
and realize where
daddy's been
six days a week

2. The Drinker

you're home
and i'm still awake
dreading your shout
pulling me on tip-toes
to see you draped
on wood fingers bracing
crazed eyes and mouth
that stink over a
tightened hand

3. Scholarship Winner

knowing i work
hard and well
my teachers guide
my artwork
into a big
illinois competition that

wins me a scholarship
to the prestigious
chicago institute of art

my proud mother
takes me to register
and the lady
mumbles oh
just a minute
before she
returns with a man
smiling like a wolf

i'm very sorry
he says
clumsy
record keepers
should've seen
someone else
really won

4. Kitchen Debutantes

they're pretty
tough and
mean those
kitchen debutantes
but i go up there
anyway

one's in a sleeveless
dress ready to fall
looking at herself
the other's tits push
open her bathrobe

hi ladies i say

Paint it Blue

they don't reply
preferring a mirror
and dirty streets
below

5. History of Negro Press

this hard ass
detective agency
needs to know
how the bleep
someone loses a history of
the negro press mural
nine feet by twenty
pulsing with a pioneer publisher
revolutionary editor and hungry
reporters photographers and pressmen
demanding to communicate

6. Nat Turner Views Mural

i poke nat turner and
say hey isn't that you
holding a torch in the mural
and he says doesn't look
much like me
but i think
most people understand
god made me
his prophet and after
that black hand
covered the sun
i knew it was time

silently with hammers and
axes we battered children

wives and their men
to free as many
slaves as we could
and kill more whites
to teach them the truth
which at the time
was my getting
hanged decapitated
and quartered
with two hundred
others

who inspired
southern legislation
preventing slave education
and right of assembly
flaying
the first amendment
which ultimately
didn't matter
since
they heard me
and nobody's forgotten

Paint it Blue

7. Drafted

am planning a mural
on blacks in big war
when the draft
attacks in forty-four
to throw me and others
chest deep into flooding
mississippi and ohio river
stench
lifting sandbags fails
to inoculate me from tb
which rips my lungs
out of the army
into the hospital
for two years reading
without paint

8. Two Alone

we're
only
two
but
un-alone
inside
my
embrace

George Thomas Clark

9. Mater Dolorosa

mater
dolorosa
tired
and
sad
leave
that
frame

10. Duel in Mexico

my creative
wife elizabeth
catlett and i
go to mexico
to work with
great muralists
and she meets
handsome printmaker
pancho while i
seethe she swears
he's teaching her
spanish and he's
learning English
but back in
new york she
says adios

Paint it Blue

11. Released

two years in
tb hospital
can't do much
except cough and
feel my wife
embrace another
as they marry
i'm hospitalized
another year
so contagious
everyone flees
except frances

helps me heal
and urge hostess
to invite her
to my freedom
party from detroit
to chicago she
travels and days
later we rush
into my apartment
alone

12. Freeport

thanks
for
breaking
the
noose
and
drawing
my
torch

George Thomas Clark

13. Blues Singer

listeners
behold
a woman
surrounded by
heat in an
armored dress
unable to
protect a head
tutored by drinks
and punches a
blues singer
needs

14. Sharecropper

i'm weary under
a sun so hot
i cool a little
touching the leaf
of a plant
that binds me
to the field

15. Southern Exhibitions

around nineteen fifty
university of alabama
presents paintings
by prominent negro
artists and informs
us in advance
we can't view
our work

Paint it Blue

when delgado museum
in new orleans
hangs one of mine
i excitedly go
to see a man
at the door
who says you've
already seen it
and will again
on colored day

16. Who're You?

sometimes
my wife and i
must ease apart
hoping they don't
understand broken
words

17. Career Change

new york tb
smokes last lung and
two months later
still can't stand
when doctor says
got to move
okay then Connecticut
no that's about same
try somewhere dry
maybe los angeles
where never rains
and everyone's
creative

George Thomas Clark

18. Pasadena Hospitality

happy here in sunny
mountain lined pasadena
guarded in our home
by neighborly police
and firefighters
who call my wife's
supervisors to protest
she's married to
one of those and
from hallowed kent
street they begin
to move

19. Birmingham Totem

from charcoal
and ink
i emerge bare
and shrouded
by debris
as softly
my hands
probe
a birmingham
church

20. Son of John Brown

vital to clarify
i don't draw
john brown
as a negro
he just comes out
that way

Paint it Blue

in charcoal and
do not move
to rising hill
road in altadena because
the liberator's son
owen brown
presides still
a-mouldering in
his grave atop
beautiful brown mountain
near our street

there fran and
i live after
adopting two
children a girl of
ethopian students
and boy from black
and chinese parents
we love the view
and our family
hikes into nature
and rejoices
most neighbors behave
but if not ill
i might kill
the man whose
hose squirts
my little girl

21. Runaway Slaves

i'm not
your faceless
female slave
melting into
confederate stars

on a wanted poster
i'm staring
at you
as i stand
breasts firm
and untouched
guarding the girl
who cringes
below

22. Sheltering Harriet

harriet taubman
harriet anyone
my aunt harriet
flees north
blanketed under
blood eyes
wary on
you

23. Daughter in Law

mother marsh says
push my wheelchair
slower
push it faster
get those flies
out of my face
so i don't have to
swat all the time
find something else
on tv
i need another cup of coffee
with more sugar
bring me ex lax
uh oh

Paint it Blue

now i'll need a bath
get the water running

silently i celebrate
when mother marsh
returns to chicago
and pray she
stays her stroke
soon threatens
a return charlie
worrying i'll let
her a second stroke
spares having to
say no way

24. Smoke

video in sunny
hollywood hill gallery
recalls seventy-seven
exhibit here featuring
charles white artwork
and interview skin
collapsing from bony
face he rasps about ideas
art and decries even
concept of death then
takes another puff

25. Devil Returns

in seventy-seven i chair otis
art college drawing and
shoulder more meetings than
know exist and keep teaching
classes and painting even as
i sleep very little preparing
exhibitions and being father

and say sure i'll paint a mural
honoring mary mcleod bethune
daughter of slaves who cherished
learning and forever charmed and
twisted for funds founding a
school that became a university
and who i portray as queen

between a young man playing
guitar and a studious woman
fronted by their child holding
a big book i work for love and
little money in bethune public

Paint it Blue

library tired as hell finishing
early in seventy-eight

that spring i rush to dresden
representing united states at
international art conference
and in fall advise howard u
grad students in washington
dc three days a month while
finishing art for big gallery
show in los angeles and before

christmas am gasping coughing
and can't rise from bed but tell
doctor i've suffered too long in
hospitals and refuse to return till
he says i'll otherwise die of
chronic obstructive pulmonary
disease in days am back home
weakening

and start seventy-nine taking
medical leaves from otis and
howard and returning to hospital
and going home bearing portable
oxygen tank soon replaced by
three oxygen tanks and more
hospitalization but back home
tanks don't help anymore

next time ambulance attendants
push my wheelchair i grab
favorite hat and say this'll bring
good luck don't worry in hospital
i try to say through oxygen mask
but can only move eyes and sleep
this mask is choking me on my back
i shoot sitting up in bed yank it off to

vomit a cup of blood my wife
catches with cupped hands

Jacob Lawrence Frees John Brown

God has chosen me and solemnly I mount the cross and for decades sacrifice to fund sacred work. In poverty I pray and tell my children only the sword will suffice and this I reveal to trusted others who understand slave chasers must perish by broadswords we wield in guerilla war. Almighty God demands I remain unfazed despite blood money on my head and next free negroes and train them and other good men to assault the federal armory at Harper's Ferry. In an old barn we load guns for many liberators but only twenty-one angels appear to help seize a hundred thousand rifles for eager black hands on our planned march into the South that's blocked by troops surrounding the armory. At least die like a man I tell my wounded son, I will too after my Virginia trial consigns me to a rope.

Notes from Heaven: Most honored I am that my eighteen fifty-nine defeat was orchestrated by Virginia's greatest son Robert E. Lee and led to my execution witnessed by brave Stonewall Jackson and dashing actor John Wilkes Booth.

George Thomas Clark

Tulsa Riots

It's May thirtieth, 1921 and I'm a teenage shoeshiner entering a large downtown Tulsa building, anxious to use the "colored" restroom on the top floor. I hurry into the elevator, trip, and to avoid falling grasp the arm of a teenage white girl whose screams send me running out. Next day I'm arrested and jailed atop the courthouse and hundreds of white citizens, enraged by street talk and inflammatory newspaper stories, mass outside and threaten to storm the jail and serve justice. Black citizens, though less numerous, arm themselves and rush to support a sheriff who promises nothing will happen. Since there've been numerous recent lynchings in Oklahoma, most blacks are skeptical.

Fearing a "negro uprising" whites hurry home for guns and get more in the local armory, and respective mobs confront each other within hours. Both swear others fire first. Moot point. Someone generally shoots when mobs collide. Whites have more firepower, take the offensive, and realize this is their cherished opportunity to burn Greenwood, the Black Wall Street, one of most affluent African American neighborhoods in America. Many homes and businesses soon glow. Police abandon civic duty and either shoot or detain blacks.

By morning on June first few residents are free to protect Greenwood. While whites loot and burn homes, some golden World War One biplanes, cockpits open to the wind, hold pilots who hurl incendiaries and pump bullets into houses engulfed by flames. On the ground more fire is applied. Twelve hundred houses and thirty-five blocks burn. Under embers most victims are black, perhaps three hundred. National Guard units race in from Oklahoma City, disarm whites, send them home, and herd blacks into internment centers. No charges are filed against me, and I'm hustled out of town and never go near Tulsa again.

The local economy soon tanks so white employers sign papers for release of workers who must wear green tags, like stars later borne by European Jews. The Red Cross offers tents and food for several thousand displaced blacks anxious to rebuild. Whites quickly craft strict building codes designed to preclude recovery and steal abandoned land. A black attorney counters with a legal challenge

128

that succeeds. But there's no financial compensation. The grand jury declares blacks brought this on themselves, and no white ever goes to prison.

The riot is rarely discussed in Oklahoma schools and later most people don't know. Some now learn in a painting of a golden biplane titled: *Tulsa Race Riot of 1921* by Curtis James. Somewhere there must also be a painting of a neighborhood reconstructed several years later.

Tobacco: The Holdouts

I'm no prude just clean-living Robert Colescott and resent unhealthy intrusions such as smoke choking me in museum gallery.

"Put out all cigarettes," I demand of unseen culprits. "Where are you?"

Dashing around gallery, I cough and curse and am about to flee when I realize I'm next to evildoers and see mummified doctor's insane teeth clinch cigarette as businessman chomps pipe, granite skull smokes cigar, tobacco picker sucks short one, boy and girl delight in puffs, weary woman dangles stick over book, sexy couple holds fire in fingers and lips, all soothed and sedated tobacco holdouts.

"Fools," I shout. "Put out damn cigarettes."

"Light up or get hell out," doctor replies.

"I'll never paint you again," I say.

The New Jemima

no more
am i
fat-faced
mammy
smiling to please
with heaps
of pancakes
oozing butter
on bacon
in my veins
i'm new
jemima
pretty and
smiling real
in your kitchen
my machine gun
spraying pancakes
soon sweetened
by a syrupy
grenade

Note: Joe Overstreet painted *The New Jemima* in 1964.

George Thomas Clark

Jacob Zuma Demands

I am "shocked and feel personally offended and violated" by the racist painting *The Spear* by white artist Brett Murray who portrays me like Lenin in a suit but with my penis exposed. This is not political satire, like an opponent says, but a form of "hate speech," as one proud daughter notes.

I know the joke. Which daughter? Which son? I'm not going to give her name, though it's already published, because this assault on my dignity also decreases her security and that of my other children.

"How many do you have?" people want to know.

I should tell them nobody's business. I've already acknowledged siring twenty and won't waste time disputing I may have three dozen or so. Understand, I've been married six times and currently maintain four wives who realize their man of energy and prestige requires vigorous outlets many women are delighted to provide.

I guarantee the 2005 rape charge was fabricated, and during the trial I often sang "Bring Me Your Machine Gun" in Zulu. People empathized. I had not been like a father to the daughter of a deceased political ally. I'd been an intimate friend, and was shocked she claimed I forced. Indeed, in cavalier fashion, I accommodated her. "In Zulu culture you cannot leave a woman if she's ready. That would've been tantamount to rape." Of course I was acquitted and the woman fled South Africa.

In a country besieged by AIDS, and a thirty-percent HIV rate, many saints declared even if I hadn't raped I was a bad role model, bedding a woman I knew HIV positive. Don't worry. I showered afterward and that surely washed everything away.

Since 2009 I've been president of South Africa and father of my country. No family head should be exposed to degradations like *The Spear*. I frankly applaud two patriots, one white and one black, who walked into a gallery and painted an X over my face and another on my genitals and smeared black paint over the obscene work. They were protecting their leader and defending dignity. You'd want same for yourself.

Europe and America

George Thomas Clark

Cave Painter

Twenty thousand years ago in a cave I said you guys bore me, forever painting stags, equines, and other critters. Look at this. A few closed around me, smirking, and I said you can't paint anything you don't see and you can't paint people and above all you can't paint people engaged with animals. My stags are elegant and free like birds flying toward four slender archers vertically aligned as they fire arrows still alive on the wall of a cave.

The Young Ribera

I am both surprised and honored to be invited to the distinguished Prado National Museum in Madrid to comment on some thirty of my paintings in an exhibition titled *The Young Ribera.* Initially I worried I might be disheartened by work I created in my early twenties, about four hundred years ago, and hadn't seen since my demise in 1652. Gratefully I can report that my portraits of everyday people reveal more about the characters than I had realized, and must thank curators at the Prado for displaying these works on a prominent wall next to the gallery entrance. This aesthetically bold decision in essence declares that my larger and more celebrated paintings of ethereal creatures, though visually pleasant and technically sound, are detached from this world and less noteworthy. *Saint Paul* and Jesus Christ commanding Lazarus to rise from the grave, in *The Raising of Lazarus,* are thus superseded by two indigent men and a fellow who overindulges.

In *A Beggar,* painted when I was twenty-one, I present a balding, haggard, and bloated man with a bulbous red nose and scraggly beard. To an indifferent world he supplicates with hat in hands. The man in *Smell* wears a ragged hat and tattered shirt and doubtless emits an unpleasant odor intensified by the onion he cuts making his eyes tear. And look at that fellow in *Taste.* He's the epitome of excess. His pudgy face bears flushed cheeks and the guarantee he shovels too much food and drink into a widening body that'll soon fail him. He's real. He's relevant. And more memorable than a saint.

George Thomas Clark

Renoir Rebukes

I had misgivings about allowing my work to be displayed in Los Angeles. True, the geography is wonderful and the women beautiful but while this city of creative souls is rife with devotees of my work, it is also crawling with libidinous louts who, I must tell you in contemporary parlance, wouldn't stop hitting on my models. I myself may have occasionally engaged in this activity, though only with those of an appropriate age. Many Angelinos should be so restrained.

At the Los Angeles County Museum of Art's gala opening of *Renoir in the Twentieth Century*, which offered many of my paintings from the 1890's and beyond, I was immediately tempted to assault a thirtyish, sunglasses-indoors fellow who suggested the lass from *Bather in Long Hair*, who in my "outdoors in studio" style appears to be standing in water, should accompany him to a private beach north of town.

"Can you not see the girl has only the beginning of pubic hair?" I said. "Away from her or I'll at once summon the authorities."

The next satyr was more outrageous still, first ogling then squeezing the shoulders of the two quite underage *Young Girls at Piano*. These ready-to-blossom creatures will undoubtedly be beautiful women but not for at least another year or two. With my chest I bounced the sly septuagenarian away from the girls. He later tried to reinvade but already-alerted museum personnel muscled him into an elevator and confined him with abstract works on the floor above.

I could not accuse the next heathen, easily in his fifties, of criminal intent when he placed a hand on the wrist of the winsome young lady in *Gabrielle and Jean*. Gabrielle Renard is mature at age seventeen but also my wife's cousin and, more importantly, the nanny of my baby son Jean.

"I think the young lady fancies me," he said.

"She's utterly devoted to my family, and in particular to Jean."

"You have a great many restrictions."

Reluctantly, I nodded toward the *The Great Bathers*, two rosy and voluptuous women in recline.

"Come," I said. "Do you speak French?"

Calling Winslow Homer

I know Winslow Homer's cell phone is turned on. It better be. He's put me in *The Gulf Stream* on a lifeless boat, without rudder and mast, where I'm leaning back, propped up by an elbow on deck, and looking resignedly away from several huge sharks converging and snapping as they ready to devour me.

Homer, is that you? Get me outta here. I don't care you're making a statement about the travails of Negroes being recently-freed but not-really-free former slaves. You stand here and make the statement. Hold up a sign.

I don't need a tropical storm. I'm trying to survive while you get paid to paint pictures and have your ass kissed. Great, you can't get here soon enough. I'm not surprised. You're a scrawny fellow. So what the hell are you gonna do? I'm not the only one who complained, you say? Some rich white viewers at the first exhibition of this painting also regretted my lack of hope. I regret it more, Homer. Please. Do something now. Mix the damn paint. What's that? A schooner way in the background. I can barely see it. And, with angry clouds and worsening waves as the storm readies to return, those on board won't be able to see me, either.

Homer, paint that boat closer to me. What's the matter with you? Do you hear me? Now my phone's dead. Service in 1899's no damn good.

George Thomas Clark

Thomas Eakins Gets Physical

I'm honored the renowned Los Angeles County Museum of Art is presenting a major exhibition of my work entitled *Manly Pursuits: The Sporting Images of Thomas Eakins.* With a substantial, though not entirely toxic, level of bitterness I must inform you that such recognition was rarely forthcoming during my lifetime, and then quite late in my journey. Collectors and critics also usually rejected my work for, in essence, being too much like real life, too emotionally evocative, and too little like the phony parlor portraits that flattered subjects and gorged the bank accounts of compliant artists who painted them.

This exhibition, though not as comprehensive as the one-hundred-fifty work showing in Paris, Philadelphia, and New York several years ago, is ideal in subject matter. I was an unabashedly physical man and will elaborate as I walk you by some of the most powerful works here today. Let us move in chronological order, starting in 1871 with my first sports painting, *Max Schmitt in a Single Scull.* Max was a champion rower in Philadelphia, and I accordingly place him in the forefront on the splendid Schuylkill River which mirrors scull and rower as well as trees to the left and a hill with trees to the right. Max has stopped rowing and is looking at you, and in the distance you'll note two elegant bridges, and between them and Max there's a broad-shouldered fellow rowing away and on his stern in red it says: Eakins.

I also swam and sailed and ice skated and wrestled and performed gymnastics, and studied drawing and anatomy at the Pennsylvania Academy of the Fine Arts, and witnessed cadavers and dissections at Jefferson Medical College, and for four years starting in 1866 I lived in Europe, primarily Paris, and learned from masters of realism. In 1876, at age thirty-two, I returned to the Pennsylvania Academy and taught in enlightened ways hidebound colleagues could not understand: in order to help my students, male and female, learn to paint the human body, I insisted on using nude male and female models in all studio classrooms. This should have been my prerogative since I'd become the academy director in 1882. I don't think nudity was ever the primary issue. Paying prostitutes or maids a dollar to disrobe had been an effective, and generally accepted, means of promoting creativity and realism. But when I started seeking more shapely and intelligent specimens, the students themselves, I heard whines and later barks from Victorian hypocrites among faculty, students, and parents of students.

Right here we have *Swimming*, an 1885 example of the vigor wrought by my academic techniques. Following a day of swimming with friends and students in a creek, and producing numerous preparatory photos and oil sketches, I painted five beautiful naked young men in fluid sequence. The lad on the left, reclining on his side on a rock, leads to the next fellow, sitting as he gazes into the water at my red dog Harry, and flows into the third young man, blessed with a particularly fine back, buttocks, and legs, looking the other direction, toward the end of the creek and the reflection of bright green grass and trees, and prompts the fourth man to dive into the creek. The youngest lad, with hair red as Harry's, is standing in the creek as my dog examines him. I'm in the right foreground, swimming toward Harry and the boys.

This is how artistic people should live. The man married to my youngest sister refused to put his accusations on paper but spread salacious rumors at the academy and elsewhere that I walked around my house, wearing shirt tails and nothing else in front of my nieces and that I'd had "incestuous and bestial" relations with my niece, his daughter, who was unable to comment because of her death. Some of my female students complained that I told them obscene jokes. Others claimed I was "aggressive and predatory" in the manner I asked them to pose naked. Several models said I touched them too much, and one lady stated I dug my fingers into her chest as she posed. That's true. I needed to feel her bones. When another female student asked me about the movement of the male pelvis, rather than struggling with some sterile academic explanation, I merely took her into my studio, pulled down my pants, and enlightened her. In that sprit, to students and friends, I often gave a photo of a nude female model serenely reclining in my arms high above my penis.

Susan, a former student and my wife of two years, understood my aesthetic destiny, but my enemies at the Pennsylvania Academy did not, and forced me out the door in 1886. Thankfully, many of my students formed the Art Students' League of Philadelphia, and there I worked as well as at schools in New York and Washington, D.C. In 1898, at age fifty-four, I gave up teaching to conserve my waning time and energy for more ambitious works than I'd been painting.

Here is one of my proudest results: *Taking the Count.* Don't stand too close. This work is about eight-feet high and seven wide, the second largest I ever painted. I wanted viewers to feel what I felt attending three hundred boxing matches. In this painting you'll see what's there, a ground floor and two balconies of male spectators, two ropes around the brown surface of the ring, a calm boxer, his right arm cocked as he studies the opponent he's knocked down, a tuxedo-clad referee (and friend of mine) examining the downed fighter, and the man on the floor, not taking the full count, but looking straight ahead, still aware, his right knee on the canvas and left foot planted and ready to push him to his feet. What you don't see but feel is the punch that knocked the man down and the punch that will soon knock him out. Naturally, this work, which I can see is moving you, did not particularly impress critics, collectors, or curators of the day.

Over here, also from 1898, we have *Salutat,* a smooth world champion, his gloves removed, saluting the crowd of well-dressed gentlemen as ethereal light illuminates a thin, chiseled back, shapely buttocks largely unobscured by a loincloth, and long, sleek legs.

And here is *Wrestlers* from 1899. My own days of grappling were at this point decades past but I visited gyms, talked to wrestlers and their coaches, took photographs, and hired models to stage this scene of manly contact. The grappler on top is attacking the man on his side, pushing his chest into the other's, crossing the T, and has thrust his right hand between the opponent's legs and under the left to clamp the right wrist. And with his left arm he's reached under the downed man's left armpit and grabbed the back of his neck, a hold that won't be broken by the downed man's alarmed attempt to reach back and remove the hand. As in *Taking the Count,* you don't see the vital take down that occurred before the image or the pin that is imminent.

Notes: Unable to attract any appropriate offers for *Swimming,* Thomas Eakins housed the painting for the rest of his life. He died in 1916 at age seventy-one. In 1990 *Swimming* was sold for $10 million. In 1876, during the Centennial of the United States, Eakins' masterly fusion of surgery, lecture, and drama, *The Gross Clinic*, was criticized when not ignored and sold for a paltry $200 to Thomas Jefferson University. In 2006 Jefferson accepted a $68 million offer for the painting but some local institutions and private donors raised the money to keep the painting in the city, at the Philadelphia Museum of Art and the Philadelphia Academy of Fine Arts.

Susan Macdowell Eakins, who dedicated much of her time to her husband's career, resumed intensive painting after Eakins' death. Her work was noteworthy, and in 1973, thirty-five years after she died, she was honored with her first one-woman exhibition at the Pennsylvania Academy of Fine Arts, where her husband had taught for ten years prior to his dismissal.

George Thomas Clark

George Luks Knocked Out

Stick with me and you'll have a great time. I'm alive and witty and drinking plenty and proud to tell you I'm a real American artist and tired of too many dollars going for European art which is fine but no better than mine and probably not as good. How could it be? Those guys aren't on stage in 1932 telling you that in their youth, at the birth of the century, they were called Chicago Whitey, a real tough boxer owning a punch so feared I called it Lame-'em Luks.

Don't you believe me? Short and pudgy I may be, and lit up I usually am in glowing print clothes and capes and large fedoras all set off by a monocle attached to my vest with a satin ribbon. I tell you I know the people on the streets and did years before I divorced my second wife and lost our large home in the Bronx and started carousing Manhattan alleys when drunk and was often taken in by my brother who ran a place for guys like me. We deserve the best.

You've probably seen my recent work. It's selling well. It's selling better than the superior work I did in 1905. Take a look at *The Spielers*. Aren't those two pretty young girls loose and joyous and alive dancing cheek to red cheek? No wonder many have called it one of the ten best paintings in American history. And how about *Hester Street*? I offer all the details of European superficiality while giving you whiskers, sloppy mustaches, unkempt beards, big noses, awkward dresses, crowded streets, and dirty buildings. I hand you a ticket straight inside. And a year later in *The Café Francis* I know you feel glee like that sophisticated geezer with bushy mustache as he teases the coat on shoulders of his voluptuous young lady.

I also love boxing matches where men prove they're men, where so often I showed myself to be Chicago Whitey standing over another victim of Lame-em Luks, my powerful right cross, or perhaps it's my diabolical left hook. It doesn't matter. Examine *The Boxing Match* from 1910. Some say I base it on Jim Jefferies, the Great Old White Hope, coming out of retirement to get slaughtered by powerful young Jack Johnson. I say not really since I've chosen a much leaner white man than still pudgy Jeffries. And rather than crumpling to the canvas like big Jeff, this very-white man in black trunks is flying to the floor as his conqueror stands poised as a panther.

Paint it Blue

Goddamn it, give me a drink. You New Yorkers don't support me and my talented buddies, painters of life you can smell and feel. I want a whiskey right now. Put me down. I've got more to say. The audience loves me, most of it. They're booing you European-licking snobs more than me. I'll bring out Lame-em Luks, I warn them, and the guy in the 1933 bar. A few hours later the police find me half dead in the street then real dead but soon celebrated at my funeral and in the press that remembers when I painted more and better and drank less.

George Thomas Clark

McSorley's Cats Soothe John Sloan

I'm shy and nervous and can't get much from women except in brothels where they'll at least pay attention awhile. In 1898 I meet Dolly at my regular place and suddenly feel I have a chance, maybe I can relax with this woman and really have her, away from here. We start going together right away. She's my girl. I've got to keep this feeling so tell Dolly not to worry she's an alcoholic. She says she's an ex-alcoholic. But sometimes she drinks and everything's rotten but I promise her I won't leave. I'll always stay and help her. I know her moods are terrible at times but we'll work it out. That's the key. I know. My father broke down when I was sixteen and I had to go to work to support the family. Father never got better but maybe Dolly will. Of course she will. This great doctor has helped by telling me to keep a diary of all the wonderful things about her. Look at your qualities, I tell Dolly, you don't need to drink tonight. And please don't say those things whether or not you drink.

I get out a lot. I have to make a living. I go where life is most vibrant, the loud and lovely streets of New York City where I paint energetic people walking and talking and eating in restaurants and drinking in saloons. I paint everything I can but am frustrated colleagues like Robert Henri, William Glackens, and George Luks are so much faster and Henri says I paint like the "past participle of slow." But these guys and lots of other people keep assuring me I'm really good though I'm forty and have only sold three paintings and have to work as a newspaper and magazine illustrator. Even after a break in 1913, at age forty-two, when a rich collector buys a painting, I need another job and become an art teacher who tells students the truth in straight language they sometimes resent but I respond with more frankness: "I have nothing to teach you that will help you to make a living." They're impressed Henri, Glackens, Luks, and others and I are known as The Eight and use an energetic and sweaty realist style some call the Ashcan School, a term I hate and warn students not to use again in front of me.

I need to relax. My favorite place is McSorley's Old Ale House on Seventh Street in Manhattan. Five times I paint this saloon renowned for "good ale, raw onions, and no ladies." We don't need women here. We have tough men who work with their hands and

Paint it Blue

Wall Street sharpies and clever journalists. Look at some of us in my favorite, *McSorley's Cats*, 1929. In the lower left I'm the guy wearing glasses, smoking a pipe, and sitting at a table that includes a cartoonist. Standing full-bellied and elegantly-suited at the bar is a prominent critic. You can smell this pungent place and see it's where to down a few and talk about anything as long as it's exciting. And look over there to the right. I know, you've seen him already. He's big John McSorley, the earthy owner, dignified in a bar apron, surrounded by his hungry cats ready to devour his generous offering of ground bull's liver.

Notes: John Sloan co-founded the Society of Independent Artists, which gave great Mexican artists Diego Rivera and Jose Clemente Orozco their first show in the United States in 1920.

Sloan's marriage to Dolly endured forty-two years until her death from heart disease in 1943. Sloan remarried and died in 1951 at age eighty.

George Thomas Clark

Walt Kuhn at the Circus

I worry too much about painting and supporting my family even before 1925 when a duodenal ulcer almost kills me. Following interminable recovery I try teaching art again and still don't like it but get relief going to the circus.

In a 1926 *Dressing Room* I paint a dark-eyed, tough-looking, rouge-cheeked sexy woman in a bathing suit that boasts her flexing biceps tightened by hands locked behind her head. I enjoy muscles and show big ones a few years later in *Top Man* who has the intimidating body of a heavyweight wrestler but is a trapeze artist who by his knees hangs upside down and uses strong arms and hands to catch flying colleagues assured that his tough, introspective face is a window to care and calculation. In 1935 the *Chorus Captain* doesn't need big muscles because she's grimly pretty with faraway eyes, red lips, pink cheeks, and a huge pink plume on her head enhancing a darker pink halter top that reveals sleek arms and a smooth tummy.

In the mid 1940's as I approach seventy I paint a striking *Green Pom-Pom* girl with ominous sexy blue eyes and red lips almost puckered. She wears a tall ornate black hat a little shorter than those in marching bands and her luminous light-brown hair touches sweet shoulders that frame breasts pointed in a revealing white top. This is all so satisfying I find I don't like to talk much anymore. I had been quite a talker, and in 1913 was a key organizer of the *Armory Show* of modern art in New York City that attracted two hundred thousand viewers and many buyers, proving Americans were not philistines. Nowadays I'm tired of trying to show and sell my work and really just want to go to the circus. When the Ringling Brothers Circus arrives I'm there every night. In 1946 I give scull-capped Roberto thick white makeup that suggests a dignified ghoul boasting muscles that surge through a pink sleeveless shirt matching pink tights. A couple of years later *Chico in a Hat* wears sharp makeup to emphasize finely-carved features and smoldering eyes.

I don't want to go home, I tell my family. The circus is home and the lives of the people I paint are really my life. I refuse to go to the hospital. You can't make me. You shouldn't. You won't get away with it for long. In 1949 an ulcer perforates and I'm gone.

Night Court

Hell, I've got no job and neither do millions of others so we can't get into court during the day and are herded in at night. The clerk in a visor's numbed by years logging all this, and the bailiff in a corner's bored as hell. Look at the judge, a fat unpleasant bastard. And the prosecutor uses his hooknose to open people like tin cans. They ought to take it easy. Nobody in night court's done much. The toothless man looking down is probably here for public drunkenness. That's fine, streets are home. The skeletal man staring straight into nothing might have snatched a chicken in a market. I hope he got to eat some. The guy with face in hand, I bet he grabbed someone's blanket last night. It was damn cold in the park. I'm the youngest and healthiest guy here. Depression hasn't gotten me down. I just pushed the bastard who hired me to clean his warehouse and then paid half what he promised.

Note: *Night Court* is a 1938 painting by Phil Paradise.

George Thomas Clark

Munch on Canvas

Self-Portrait, 1881-1882

surprised
handsome
in
late teens
expected
tight jaw
and
eyes
tunneling
turmoil

Despair

thoughts
of faceless
man fall
into frigid
hole pushed
by dead
water beneath
sky bleeding
more blank
faces

Evening on Karl Johan Street, 1892

hate
walking on
karl johan
street
stampeded
by cold-eyed

Paint it Blue

people

Death in the Sickroom, 1893

tired of
sick people
dying tired
of seeing
people
sickened by
death tired
of being sick
tired of waiting
for death
disgusted
haven't
grabbed it

The Scream, 1894

inherent
scream
seizes
frantic
head
between
desperate
hands

Anxiety, 1894

fiery
skies
on
cold

days
hurl
faces
reflecting
what
desperate
to
avoid

Kiss, 1897

face
melted
into
hers
where
couldn't
breathe

The Dead Mother, 1899-1900

dead
mother
peaceful
in bed
little
girl
wide
eyed
in
pit

Paint it Blue

Self-Portrait in Hell, 1903

hell
no
redder
than
face
pity
will
survive

Self-Portrait (in distress), 1919

walls
furniture
jumpy
and
skewed
as van
gogh's
but
head
still
not
ready
to shoot

George Thomas Clark

The Artist and his Model, 1919-1921

enter
studio
to see
young
model
relaxed
in open
bathrobe
blue in
front of
suit and
tie close
to messy
blue bed

Self Portrait. The night wanderer, 1923-1924

ever
awake
hear
steps
rise
and
look
into
darkness

Paint it Blue

Self-Portrait. Between the clock and the bed, 1940-1943

spindly
eighty
rejoice
clock to
right
prepares
sturdy
bed
on left

George Thomas Clark

Munch Scores

For record hundred twenty million they just sold *The Scream* one of four and last in public hands and I'll burn all of them including money and hands if they ever make me look inside myself again.

Is that Matt Damon

My painting is one of the smallest works in the museum at Stanford University, and I'm one of the least celebrated artists on the premises. Pablo Picasso and Diego Rivera have infinitely more renown, and so do Rodin and his monumental sculptures of introspective people. In this company, my *Self-Portrait with Small Statue* is understandably tucked behind an obscure exhibition wall in a corner of the museum. I was only twenty-three in 1911 when I painted it, and had just returned from traveling and studying in London and Paris to teach art at my alma mater here in Palo Alto. What I couldn't have foreseen is that the blond young man on my canvas looks strikingly like a famous actor who would follow me a few generations later.

I wonder how many have noticed my resemblance to Matt Damon. It's as if the actor had been sent back a hundred years so I could paint him. I know he'd like to own this piece. He could certainly afford it. Actors now earn more in a day than I did in a year, and I was usually a solvent fellow, though by no means rich. Wondering how I'd be doing in the market today, I recently (and quite anonymously) called a gallery in New York that represents my work. The friendly lady told me that my *Self-Portrait with Amaryllis* is a fine buy at forty-five thousand dollars. Even adjusted for inflation, that's quite complimentary. In this work, incidentally, I appear as a distinguished and rather stern middle-aged gentleman who no longer resembles Matt Damon, though we'll have to wait another generation to discover how he changes.

Those familiar with the beauty and tranquility of Stanford and the hills and trees in surrounding areas may be amazed that I elected to leave the university after serving in Europe in World War One. I was allured by the independence of living in a small art colony in scenic Hudson River Valley about forty-five minutes by car from New York City. My first tasks were to design a home then personally build it in the woods with the help of one local man. I called my stone place Crow House, recalling the black birds circling overhead as we worked. The residence was immediately praised for the same qualities noted more than eight decades thereafter by the *New York Times*, that the house hasn't changed and my pottery is omnipresent and most spectacularly displayed in the upstairs bathroom, an "aerie with a handmade brown, beige and black striped sink and a ceramic toilet ...as well as a tile mural of a nude on the shower wall. Downstairs (my) delicate plates, showing portraits of friends and relatives, line the shelves of a handmade cabinet...(The house) is also important because of the way (I) integrated art, as opposed to merely applying it: stair railings, doorknobs, lighting, ceramics...(I) was really the last of the great artist-craftsmen."

My friends and neighbors in the area sometimes asked me to design new homes for them or renovate what they already had, and over the decades I drew my visions on behalf of actors, entertainers, and playwrights including Burgess Meredith, Lotte Lenya, Kurt Weill, John Houseman, and Maxwell Anderson. In a 1921 letter to my friend Birger Sandzen, a painter whose works today are priced about twice as high as my own, I wrote: "I'm going to start a pottery, to do large simple decorative pieces. This to take the place of teaching as an income maker, and also to give us joy in the doing.

"The feeling of the unrelatedness of painting to our life gets me more and more, and I want to do more things than paint pictures. The joy and satisfaction in making the house has been tremendous, and the future work of carving and painting our huge beams and stones will be great.

"For the artists who like the competition for shows and publicity – let 'em have it. For me, I want to make beautiful things so as to make our living as beautiful as possible, and where humans live in swarms like ants I don't think wholesome beautiful living is possible. I truly long for the disintegration of our civilization. This (New York) city, with its miles of sky-scraping apartments, degrades human beings."

Though I wanted to make a living as an artist, and focused considerable time on my ceramic works, my aesthetic goals always superseded the financial. Even today some pottery collectors with sterile preferences condemn me with online insults like "lazy" and "red herring." And they attack me with my own words, which I believe refute them and certainly express how I still feel: "Loving drawing and painting, I follow wholeheartedly the technique which I felt demanded least technical and scientific knowledge and gave most freedom and richness to drawing and color. From the beginning I had an obsession against letting technique be the controlling factor. I even exhibited and sold cracked and imperfect pieces if I felt the decoration was fine enough, as you would mount a drawing, if you like it, even though the paper was torn and soiled...my sole criterion is still the life of each piece, and its beauty of form and decoration, not its technical perfection."

Making pottery revitalized my desire to paint on canvas, and I created numerous landscapes, still lifes, and portraits which served as tune-ups for murals in the Department of Justice and Department of Interior buildings in Washington, D.C., and those prepared me for my grandest commission, the conception and creation of *The Land-Grant Frescoes* at Penn State University. I started sketching in September 1939 and several months later in Old Main lobby began to brush paint on wet plaster prepared every morning by my daughter Anne. The centerpiece of the mural is a towering and gaunt Abraham Lincoln, gesturing with enormous hands, after he presents a sapling to a student. Lincoln had supported higher education, and the results are around him: four generations say farewell to a promising son, headed for school, as their cat slyly laps milk out of a bucket; agricultural students examine seedlings while behind them others work the land; mechanical students make machinery parts against a backdrop of Pennsylvania mines and industry; young women learn chemistry; a hulking football player stands above other athletes; and more images abound.

I continued to live in Crow House and taught at Columbia and helped found the Skowhegan art school in Maine. My daughter Anne stayed with my wife and me after our son Peter moved out, and both were there when I died in 1970, and Anne remained after my wife passed away and until her own death. Peter then inherited the house and is now being assailed by art and history lovers who believe he shouldn't have sold the house to a developer who Peter acknowledges "will change it so it's unrecognizable." That saddens me but I do not condemn Peter. He patiently waited for public funding that never materialized before he sold the place for more than a million dollars. My granddaughter Anna, who's a sculptor, wanted to raise a down payment then pay her father installments. As Peter told the *New York Times* last year, he declined because he didn't want his children to undergo "a dreadful burden...It's been sitting here for years, and what's the alternative? To sit here and watch it slowly deteriorate? The doors won't close. The latch on the studio door is inoperable. One beam is rotted away...I can't be sentimental about it."

I am sentimental about it and feel Crow House would have made a fine little museum. This is warranted since my paintings reside in major museums around the country and my murals will outlast the money poor Peter received as well as whatever structure the eager investor puts up. I doubt at this stage anything creative or farsighted will be done. Matt Damon certainly has the wherewithal to act. Perhaps I'll call him.

Note: In 2008 the town of Ramapo, New York teamed with the state to buy and save unique Crow House of artist Henry Varnum Poor from either destruction or radical renovation, but in several ensuing years Ramapo officials have done little to transform the site into an art museum, and the structure continues to deteriorate.

Mickey Walker on Canvas

I wasn't worried about losing a 1925 middleweight title decision to Harry Greb, I got a rematch a few hours later. He was in a nightclub, acting nice with two blondes, and asked me to join them. We closed the joint and I don't remember where the ladies went but Harry and I stepped outside to address mutual insults and, as he naively took off his coat, I nailed him in the kisser, knocking him back against a car. We mixed it up quite a while. As the only survivor and sole judge, I give myself a unanimous decision.

I already owned the welterweight title and usually didn't let judges, referees, or newspapermen decide who won. My left hook, about like a heavyweight's, was the only voice needed. After Greb lost his title to Tiger Flowers and died following an auto accident and operation in 1926, I decisioned Flowers in a fight most fish wrappers and other loudmouths thought I lost. Look, I knocked him on his ass in the ninth round. Ask the referee. He said Flowers was slapping, rather than hitting me, and only hurt me when he thumbed my eyes.

I beat sixteen guys in a row, stopping most, but had to figure out what to do. I was only five-seven and kept putting on muscle so decided to become light heavyweight champion. In 1929 I fought Tommy Loughran. He was a great boxer and earned the decision. I didn't cry in my beers. I drank 'em and everything else with alcohol. Prohibition didn't bother me. I had a ball. People all over wanted to meet me. I was friendly with Al Capone but would've busted his big mouth if someone hadn't stepped in. I told the guy he saved Al. He said, no, he saved my life. What the hell?

I loved to travel and have a good time, even spent fifty grand during a trip to Paris. I also loved the ladies, and they felt the same about me. I ended up marrying one woman three times and another twice and guided four women down the aisle seven times. My wives and everyone else needed to understand. My habits didn't hurt my fighting. After Loughran I won twenty-two straight and decided to become heavyweight champion of the world. First, in 1931, I needed to beat Jack Sharkey, who might've become champion his previous fight but fouled Max Schmeling. I knew I could take Sharkey. And I did, believe me. Look at the films. I was much quicker nailing his body and head. Sharkey must've gotten a sympathy draw.

I kept beating bigger guys, including heavyweights Bearcat Wright and Paulino Uzcudun, and figured I could take Schmeling, who'd been decisioned by Sharkey in his previous fight. But I confess Der Max pounded me with right-hand hammers and I felt a little small for heavyweight, getting knocked down and battered around the ring. Frankly, I was glad they stopped it after the eighth round. I moved back down to light heavyweight and fought Maxie Rosenbloom in 1933. They got it right calling him "Slapsy Maxie." I don't think he hit me hard with a fist all night. But, okay, maybe he really won. I should've stopped right there. Isn't hindsight great? I lost six times in two years and was stopped twice by guys you haven't heard of.

Several years later I won my biggest fight. I was entertaining in some nightclub and getting heckled and about to go after the guy but said to myself, wait, that idiot's exactly what I look like to others. Folks, I told the customers, everyone have a drink on me because this is the last one I'll ever take.

Geez, I felt a lot better and got more active in things. With my wife I saw a movie based on the life of Paul Gauguin and, after maybe three viewings, I said I've got to try that and went to the art supplies store and spent a couple hundred bucks and told the clerk I'd bust him if he told anyone tough Mickey Walker bought sissy stuff. Soon I wanted everyone to know I was painting. Couldn't have hidden it, anyway. Many called me an "easel addict" since I was painting ten to twenty hours at a stretch. I thought people were joking in 1944 when they offered me a solo exhibition at the Waldorf-Astoria Hotel. Experts called me primitive but that's not necessarily bad in painting. Lots of my still lifes, landscapes, and city scenes sold for good money, and I had another exhibition the following year. Old sportswriters said I should've taken off my gloves before painting, but collectors understood. I connected with scenes and could make them dark or light, happy or sad. My wife at the time grew jealous of the canvases overwhelming our house, and during our divorce called art my "mistress."

I decided to give up marriage as just another bad fight or drink and would've stayed single until Martha, a pretty blonde twenty years younger, made my heart race. We did pretty well. I'm not blaming boxing that people found me unconscious on the street when I was about seventy-three. They thought I'd fallen off the wagon or been beaten. Doctors determined I had Parkinson's disease and needed care. Several years later I finished life in a convalescent home, same place as those who had a lot less fun.

George Thomas Clark

Norman Rockwell Explains

Doggone it, I'm more than a slick salesman, or crowds three-deep wouldn't be maneuvering to view my paintings in twenty-first-century galleries and halls at Crocker Art Museum in Sacramento and lots of other places. I'm tried of artists, who can't paint recognizable faces or convey emotions or capture scenes, calling me a sugar-coated shill who paints an unreal America that never was or will be so warm and comfortable. Ignore those blabbermouths. I know what I paint is true because I feel and photograph it first.

Look at that enraptured 1924 *Boy Scout* listening to his old grandfather. Most think he's telling the lad about his Civil War adventures but in fact he's advising, "If your wisdom teeth could talk they'd say, 'Use Colgate.'" No one can refute the truth in that. Over here, from *Fruit of the Vine*, an enchanted old mother watches her grown daughter dump raisins onto a table. I'm not ashamed but proud my image induces people to eat Sun Maid Raisins. I'll bet *Market Day Special* is even more successful: grandma's serene holding up a bag of raisins and explaining their virtues, and her two beautiful granddaughters, one subtly sexy in early puberty and the other a child, are transported and so is their little dog, sitting up and raising a paw toward the table.

Don't accuse me of only promoting consumer products. I also sell war bonds better than any artist. And why not? Behold *Freedom from Want* and a delicious 1943 family arrayed around white cloth on the dining room table headed by graying pop and mom who bears a gigantic cooked turkey that four generations of relatives ignore while consuming each others' delirious grins. They know they'll always have a healthy and happy family. There'll also be eternal *Freedom of Speech*. My heroic everyman is mesmerized and almost orgasmic as he stands at a meeting and peers at liberty. Some sneer that he's as mind-controlled as a fascist. Nonsense. Show me a fascist so unabashedly wholesome.

Sometimes I like to counterpunch my critics and even paint an *Art Critic* in 1955. This scholarly young fellow, powered by aesthetic glee I concede I've never felt, and armed with a palette and easel, pulls out a magnifying glass and bends over to examine the jewelry, and bosom, of a delighted Renaissance lady ensconced in a painting wherein her flirtatious eyes beckon.

In *Triple Self-Portrait* I remind snobs that my technical skills are, shall we confess, rather superior to theirs. In this work you see my back as I sit on a stool and peer around the canvas and into a mirror at my bespectacled, pipe-holding face looking back at me, and on the canvas in between rests my serene visage sans glasses but with pipe still in place. Crowning my canvas I've placed the helmet of an ancient warrior and on my right there are, among others, motivational photos of self-portraits by Rembrandt and Van Gogh. Next time you think Norman Rockwell's a hack, try painting all that.

Next time you think I live in a vacuum, make a statement about segregation and those who violently oppose desegregation. Paint *The Problem We All Live With* and the little black girl, cute in white ribbon, dress, socks, and shoes, who walks dutifully down a sidewalk, past the tomato that just missed her head and splattered the wall, paint her walking to her new school, following and followed by two U.S. marshals, mysterious and rhythmic in suits and black shoes. Paint her walking into a new era. Paint her so decades later people three-deep stand to watch.

George Thomas Clark

Photos in Box

At first ping I leave Word, and rigors of composition, checking my inbox to see email titled "Some Very Rare Photos" that instantly evoke distant memories: Wright Brothers get their plane off ground; Titanic announces it's big, dumb, and smoky embarking on maiden voyage and, decades later, sleek and relaxed on ocean floor; break-time construction workers dangle feet off steel beam of Empire State Building; baby Adolf Hitler appears not entirely perverse but later, as Fuehrer, utterly strange staring at Pope Pius while both men shield groins with crossed hands; middle-aged and stylish Albert Einstein's comfortable surrounded by idolatrous scientists; handsome Charlie Chaplin smiles sitting next to emaciated Mahatma Gandhi; early computer sprouts wires from walls of large room; hut-like McDonalds sports sign just as big advertising fifteen-cent hamburgers; young private Elvis Presley projects sobriety and eternal sweetness; Jack Kennedy, eyes and mouth eerily open and neck wound visible, lies on slab in Dallas; smiling Che Guevara and Fidel Castro pretend not to fear each other; unrecognizable kid Osama bin Laden poses with his wealthy family in front of upscale store; nestled amid soft white upholstery Martin Luther King receives lady's gentle touch in casket; John Lennon's dashing and at ease signing autograph for Mark David Chapman; sculpted Bruce Lee, doomed as Elvis, puts arm around Chuck Norris; Berlin Wall gets axe it deserves; Pope John Paul blesses man who shot him; Google launch team celebrates in 1999; George W. Bush broods in elementary school classroom on September eleven; Saddam Hussein's fitted with noose; don't know who'll be in next photo.

Lady for Lucian Freud

brother says
he'd never do
old woman
and young
women with
old men
are gross
but i don't
care since
i'm just
modeling for
lucian freud
who's damn
good looking
for guy in
eighties

hair thick
and combed back
sophisticated gray
over patrician face
and strong body
it's cool he's
freud's grandson
who talks
about poses
he paints
making me
part of
history and
pleased he
keeps bringing

me back
to study and

revise
but fear he
may keep
painting and
decide next
time he pauses
to rip brush
away and pull
where young
women wiggle

Paint it Blue

Thiebaud in the Sky

On a summer afternoon at salty-wind-whipped Palace of the Legion of Honor in foggy northwest San Francisco, not far from the Golden Gate, I attend *Wayne Thiebaud, A Paintings Retrospective,* and am moved to return the next day when I turn to a lady and say, "Incredible."

"Not really," she says.

"You must be alluding to his most publicized works, those endless rows of pies, cakes, hot dogs, and other delights."

"I'm referring to his lack of depth."

"Are you new to viewing art?"

"I beg your pardon; I teach art at the college level. I also know Wayne Thiebaud well and play tennis with him."

A lady overhearing our conversation reaches into *Around the Cake,* takes a piece, licks the icing, and says, "Delicious. Everything Thiebaud does is superb."

"You both lack the academic grounding to understand his shallowness."

"Please come look over here," I tell the professor. The other lady stays behind, reaching for another slice. "Here we have *Girl with Ice Cream Cone,* more food, yes, but with a fine portrait of a beautiful woman – the artist's second wife – opening her sensuous mouth to a phallic cone. And, in an old one-piece swimsuit, her legs are also open and inviting. Hadn't you noticed these elements?"

"The portrait does nothing for me."

"This might help," I say, grasping the cone and biting some dark pink ice cream, and handing it to her. "Of course, I understand you can't crave a woman in the sense I do."

"In fact, I can."

"In that case please concede you'd love to join *Woman in Tub,* another moving depiction of the artist's wife."

"I'd be willing to join her, though that's in no way an artistic concession."

"Over here. Look at that *Man Sitting – Back View.* What does his face look like? What is he thinking? Why is he sitting alone like that? Why isn't he looking at the painter? Where does all that white space lead? I think he's isolated, and not just in this portrait.

"And here's *Two Seated Figures* almost side by side but physically and emotionally disconnected, arms crossed as they look into different worlds. Thiebaud also isolates these *Five Seated Figures*; despite nearness they're impervious to each other."

"You see more than I than do. Wayne doesn't claim to embody so much."

"He's notoriously modest. Check out these cityscapes. In *Ripley Ridge*, and others, Thiebaud exaggerates the road's angle of elevation leaving cars as solitary climbers on a precipice that may hurl them onto their backs. I'm not surprised no one's walking or driving on *18th Street Downgrade*. It's the edge of existence. Step close to *Apartment Hill*. Are you afraid? Atop a hill that can't be climbed the apartment soars into an ominous orange sky over a freeway jammed with cars that can only exit into an abyss.

"These cityscapes from the seventies, and the food and portraits executed in the sixties, suffice to make Wayne Thiebaud one of the finest artists of the second half of the twentieth century."

"Ridiculous."

"You probably won't concede, or haven't perceived, that Thiebaud continues growing in the nineties, in his seventies, when he paints unique aerial landscapes of the Delta. *River and Farms* is an eerie yet beautiful world of fields blue, orange, and yellow, and water creamy enough to pour onto one of his cakes. And behold *Waterland*. The valley is a luscious dessert, a forlorn place of static water, a scene I dare you to visit."

"I'm not afraid of anything Wayne Thiebaud paints," says the professor, who climbs into the landscape and disappears.

Angry Subjects of Antonio Lopez

I wish these museum visitors would stop saying I must've been the little girl in the *The Dinner* by Antonio Lopez. Granted, I'm the dour and submissive wife in *Mari and Antonio* but I assure you I had a happy childhood, well, perhaps not happy but not unhappy and definitely not traumatic or anything that troubles me still. I'm not disturbed by my husband, at least not devastatingly so. I wouldn't marry him again but had to marry someone and he was the only one there. Maybe I should've waited. Maybe someone else would've asked. Maybe another one wouldn't have hurt me. I won't hurt this one unless I have to but probably not even then. Antonio Lopez hurts him for me, blurring his hateful face as we uneasily pose together

Wait. There's that little girl sprinting past long lines and trying to charge into the Lopez exhibition at the Thyssen-Bornemisza Museum in Madrid. She won't listen and the guards are slow and she's already in front of *The Dinner*, her face here and on canvas not notably sad but suggesting sadness and, on her mother's already ruined face, she pounds both hands until guards pull her away.

George Thomas Clark

Gallery Search in Madrid

After years of studying websites, scouring maps, and making many wrong turns en route to art galleries usually difficult to park near and often closed during listed business hours, or that had secretly gone out of business, I said fuck it. I'm simply going to Bergamot Station in Santa Monica, a constellation of about thirty-five excellent contemporary spaces arrayed around a large parking lot for visitors. I wasn't absolutely dogmatic, of course. If I already knew where individual galleries were, or had reliable tips how to conveniently get there, in Los Angeles and other cities, I'd occasionally go.

In Madrid I had no option but start with a blank slate and struggle to find what people are painting now. The old works of legend are easily located along and near the Paseo del Prado where three great museums – the Prado, the Thyssen-Bornemisza, and the Reina Sofia – daily receive thousands of aficionados from around the world. The Madrid galleries I'd found online were sprawled in four different postal zones and sometimes on streets the locals I talked to didn't know.

Fortuitously, I was given a gallery guide after dining at the Hotel Ritz, and studied a map and listings that from hard experience I knew would be partially out of date. I tried to convince myself to forgo the gallery experience and just relax and almost succeeded until about three o'clock on a Friday afternoon when, spontaneously, I rebuked myself for almost ignoring a new cultural opportunity, and summoned a taxi, handed the driver the guide, and said let's go. He drove around the Chueca district, heart of Madrid's gay community. Unlike San Francisco's Castro district, a majority of people on the streets of Chueca are straight. Such matters are irrelevant. This area has the most galleries. But after running up a tab while finding two closed galleries, the driver decided to tell me they're generally open until two p.m. when they shut down before reopening at four-thirty. Only much later did I see this information listed in the guide.

Back in the hotel, with intensity and obsession that alarmed me, I looked for galleries on the same streets and wrote their addresses on blank paper, and then made another list projecting the possible order in which they should all be visited. This information I handed to a taxi driver from Bulgaria who had fifteen years experience navigating the streets of Madrid. He, too, hadn't heard of many of the streets and couldn't locate them on the gallery guide map lacking detail. Reaching for the computer navigational box on the left side of his dashboard, he typed in an address, and we took off.

The first place was open but a custom-artsy furniture store that merely hung a couple of paintings. At the next location they sold only frames and ceramics. The following place was a real art gallery, with several spacious rooms on the second floor, but the show had recently closed and walls were bare. Each time I hustled into a place to make these determinations, the driver either waited out front, if law permitted, or drove around the block, the meter ever running.

"Are you rich?" he asked.

"No, I just really like looking."

Finally, we started finding some action: another second-floor gallery was loaded with fine large abstract paintings, one offered some good contemporary depictions of streets and people, another was showing photos by the late, renowned photographer of homoerotic subjects, Robert Mapplethorpe. His most stunning pieces featured a man who can hang with horses. I dashed up and down streets and stairs and around corners and waved to the driver or he to me and at the end of this quick-strike operation I had about a forty-dollar tab.

Depleted by traveling expenses, I couldn't afford anything I'd seen, the least expensive of which was a small abstract painting for about five hundred dollars. That was fine. All my walls at home are covered with art, and some closets and cabinets are packed with it. Knowing I'd worked hard and accomplished something, I felt good about eight p.m. strolling on my favorite Madrid street, Calle de Fuencarral, and was surprised to note that around the corner from my hotel stood an art gallery I'd passed at least ten times without noticing. The window was blocked inside by a board or paint – that perhaps is why the place hadn't registered – and in the display area hung several excellent surrealistic paintings. The glass door was closed, and through it, at the back of the room, I saw an old lady painting.

I entered and asked if I could look around. She didn't hear what I said. I repeated my question and she smiled. This space – Arte

Gonmar – was more working studio than gallery, and scores (perhaps hundreds) of paintings were leaning against walls or stacked on the floor or tables. A huge abstract floral work hung on the rear wall.

"How much is that one?" I asked.

"Ten thousand euros," she said. That's about sixteen thousand dollars.

I must've flinched.

"No one paints surrealism like me. Where are you from?"

I told her.

"I've been to the United States many times, and taught and lived in Mexico, and no one there does work like this."

I examined her extraterrestrial world inhabited by edgy creatures, and said, "Your work is very good but there are fine artists everywhere."

In a little while she agreed. Meanwhile she kept telling me to speak up and speak Spanish. I assured her I was. After inquiring about the prices of progressively smaller works, which were still beyond my budget, I focused on post-card size and slightly larger works stacked and scattered on a table near the entrance. Almost every time I picked one up she said, "Muy bueno." And she warned "mojado," wet, when I touched pieces recently painted.

"How many have you painted today?"

"Five," she said, and handed me one.

I said, "Muy bueno," and continued my search and after an hour of looking and talking I selected one about seven by five inches she called *El Indio Mexicano*. The price of forty euros was a bargain. And the next day I returned and talked and looked for another hour and paid twenty euros for an even smaller piece called *Indian on a Horse* that looks like ET on a flying creature. I wrote out this information for my records, and she professionally signed the papers "F. Gonmar." Later I learned online that her first name is Fanny. Her age is listed as eighty, and that may be omitting a decade.

"That really is a great painting on your back wall," I said. "How long did it take to paint?

"At least two or three months."

"I think I'm going to buy it and take it home."

She smiled and said, "You couldn't get it on the plane."

Pig in Heat

Heat comes early in the Central Valley and Joe is baked awake before five a.m. and ready to sweat as he lurches onto his right shoulder then the left back and forth. The big fan above is on low and only stirs heavy air in the second-floor bedroom of his tiny townhouse, and he's too groggy to get up and change the speed. It would've been much cooler on the first and only floor of his new three-bedroom house. Everything there was better but he surrendered comfort to start a company that consumed more than produced.

Thankfully, Joe's bourgeois instincts compelled him to keep his day job. Otherwise he'd be homeless and really learning about elements. He knows he couldn't survive that. Even in a climate-controlled office downtown this morning it's too hot and he can't get comfortable and is already tired. Everyone is. It's Friday. Around noon he leaves for the day, trudging over asphalt that could fry hamburgers. Inside his car it must be one-twenty.

He's got to do something fun. He can't go straight home to his office on the second floor. Instead, he'll go to an art gallery he just learned about. Many fine paintings cover the walls. The ones he wants cost about three grand, more than his car's worth. He'll find something else. He thinks he sees it. It's a pig's face captured in loose strokes opening up the creature's soul. This is a kind and introspective pig and pretty in a porcine way. He's got to have it. He won't get a rush until he buys something. He pays a hundred fifty, puts the pig in the trunk, and heads home.

Everything's flat in the valley and today that monotony is good. Climbing mountains would be tough on a car in its mid-teens. He gets on the freeway then takes this exit for the ten-thousandth time and drives a few blocks to the usual left turn lane. But it doesn't feel right. It isn't. It's the wrong one, about a mile too soon. He's not going to sit there just to make a useless left turn. Checking his rearview mirror, he watches cars pass then pulls right into and through the intersection, glancing for police. Of course there aren't any, and there better not be any at the next intersection. All the other cars are turning left. As the light burns red he enters the turn lane and accelerates. A car entering from the left stops quickly and the driver blows his horn. Joe jerks his neck and returns fire as both men hurl unheard curses.

He won't have to deal with any more assholes. He's pulling into a garage so narrow he can barely climb out a partially open door. The floor is slippery with dirt. Joe can't get motivated to sweep this dingy space. It must be hotter in here than outside. Inside the townhouse it's ninety-two on the thermostat. After igniting the air conditioner, he hustles back into the garage and opens the trunk to retrieve the pig. Where can he hang it? Paintings already occupy every logical space. Maybe there's one place. It's in the upstairs bathroom over a towel rack. Joe pounds a nail into the wall and hangs the box canvas. This pig is a thinker and every time Joe enters the bathroom they examine each other directly or through the medicine cabinet mirror, and in a few days he feels he's starting to look like the pig and the resemblance will increase unless he hangs it in the dusty garage.

Room with Curtains

Pink blossoms on sheer curtains caress blonde woman
collapsed at base of statue opposite heroic leader immune to her
lover prone at stone feet caressed by living blue water surrounded
by pink trees and clean white gravestones on prettiest spring day
ever.

George Thomas Clark

Silicon Galleries

Art aficionado Bill walked into frame shop in Silicon Valley and asked owner, where are galleries around here?

There aren't any, he said, just places like this that make custom frames and hang few paintings.

All this wealth. Why isn't area great for galleries?

Don't quote, but there are lots of technical people.

Kinkade in Heaven

God rang the bell quite early and told a short bald man, "Here's your new roommate. Put down that brush. You'll be painting together until further notice. Now turn on the TV. I'll check on your progress directly."

"I don't watch TV."

"Turn it on."

The old man aimed enormous eyes at a pudgy, gray-goateed fellow, and activated a large flat screen revealing a face several years fresher. The *60 Minutes* interviewer asked the newcomer what he thought about Picasso.

"I don't believe, in time, that he will be regarded as the titan that he is now," he said. "He is a man of great talent who, to me, used it to create three Picassos before breakfast because he could get ten thousand dollars for each of them."

"Who the hell are you?"

"Thomas Kinkade, *Painter of Light.*"

"Wonderful, the kitchen needs a coat of glossy antique white."

"You won't be so glib after examining my portfolio," said Kinkade, opening a large leather folder that released blinding colors.

The man looked but did not speak.

"As you must surely concede, I've created a Christian paradise of cottages, churches, gardens, and street scenes that make people feel love for life and each other. You and all the critical darlings, combined, haven't sold as much art as I."

"Inside every building resembles a blast furnace, for spiritual cremations, perhaps, of the righteous millions who collect your work. How is it so many can acquire the paintings of Thomas Kinkade?"

"We have mass production techniques unimaginable in your time."

"So they're hanging posters."

"No, they're virtually indistinguishable from originals. I have hundreds of artisans reproducing my work, and 'master highlighters' apply a touch of real paint to the most expensive pieces."

"You're joking."

"You evidently wish I were."

"This isn't art. It would be too easy to call it kitsch, as I'm confident many others have. So let's refer to it as visual fatuity."

"You're jealous my art corporation some years sold more than a hundred million dollars of art, merchandise, and even cozy Kinkade housing developments."

"I love money but it's not what drives me to explore the human soul. You seem incapable of growth or change. I'm afraid it's you who're jealous."

"I carefully create each new work as a unique expression."

"They're continuations of the same painting."

"You think only the painful, the distorted, and the unfathomable are artistic."

"The alternative is illustration. Here, I'll set up an easel for you. Let's see a portrait. Can't you paint a real person?"

"You haven't painted a real person since childhood."

"Only rarely, since I mastered realism in my teens. Then I began creating otherworldly people."

Every day the artists painted several hours. Picasso coached, cajoled, and sometimes insulted his studio companion, and Kinkade's work began to deepen and portray alcoholism, depression, and marital strife. Alas, God decided this development would outrage Kinkade's evangelical base, so He assigned each artist a new roommate.

Notes: I realized, during his interview on *60 Minutes*, that Thomas Kinkade was disturbed, and troubling reports soon trickled in. He demanded that owners of Thomas Kinkade Galleries purchase more inventory than needed. If they resisted, he threatened to saturate their regions with more Kinkade Galleries. Two former associates sued, and the court awarded them seven-figure settlements. More lawsuits are pending.

Kinkade was an alcoholic who needed intensive psychotherapy and probably psychotropic medication. At a public business gathering he drunkenly grabbed a woman's breasts. After another evening of excess, he urinated on a Winnie the Pooh figure outside a motel in Anaheim. He also had a DUI in 2010. He didn't go to bed and die happily, as his girlfriend told reporters, but, as she originally informed the 911 dispatcher, he'd stayed up all night, drinking heavily.

Paint it Blue

Despite all this, I grant that Thomas Kinkade could paint a pretty commercial picture.

George Thomas Clark

The Collector

It started on a Thursday as an unhappy summer revelation in the Los Angeles art community, became a sad tale the next day in San Francisco, grew into distressing news that Sunday in New York, progressed into shocking events the following Thursday in Scottsdale, soared as an appalling series of coincidences Saturday in Sedona, and on Sunday in Santa Fe finally erupted with more than many believed could be mere tragic chance. Six of the finest young and mid-career artists in the nation had reportedly committed suicide in little more than a week, and the newspapers and news and art magazines and television and radio stations, as well as relatives and colleagues of the departed, were asking angry questions. Some even leveled accusations of the most extreme wrongdoing but offered no evidence, nor could they conceive of anything plausible. As the crescendo of details spread, police in respective jurisdictions also began to doubt a spontaneous outbreak of ultimate despair could account for so much horror in such short time.

Each case was more thoroughly examined. And the first two decedents, who thankfully had not been cremated as they'd requested, were exhumed and scrutinized by esteemed coroners and pathologists, and even one prize-winning investigative reporter. The other dead artists were still in refrigeration and each more than once pulled out and put on the slab. Scientists and detectives involved in this investigation agreed that confidentiality was mandatory and manfully exerted themselves to maintain secrecy. The investigative reporter, however, had to be jailed, for impersonating a police officer, when he revealed that the first to die, expressionistic painter Adelberto Vargas of Los Angeles, probably didn't kill himself with carbon monoxide in his car because, judging by the egg-shaped lump on his head and examination of his brain, he had likely been unconscious before entering his vehicle.

Though the glory-seeking journalist had cynically deceived authorities, he in fact rendered great service: now the nation's artists knew an unrelenting killer was after them. The artists, though a gentle lot by nature, armed themselves with pistols, rifles, switchblades, and mace, and many took their poodles and Chihuahuas to the pound and returned with pit bulls and Rottweilers.

Paint it Blue

Law enforcements officials were now cooperating with quite rare thoroughness and vigor, and soon released stunning results from their investigations. Adelberto Vargas of Los Angeles was indeed not the only artist to have died from foul play. Right up the coast in San Francisco, Josephine Bragg was a victim, like so many of her female subjects on canvas. The life of Josephine Bragg, perhaps less gruesomely, was terminated by a massive infusion of heroin. But interviews with many friends revealed she had no history of drug use and in fact abhorred any form of intoxication. Furthermore, toxicology reports proved that Bragg's system had been injected with enough heroin to kill five people, and much of that was pumped in after she had expired.

The report from the other coast was just as unsettling. Alfonso de la Torre, whose huge paintings of anguished faces had attracted a growing audience in New York, and elsewhere, had in fact not smothered himself with a plastic bag. The notion was absurd. Alfonso de la Torre was a happy man, much happier than any artist his colleagues had ever known, and was excited by career progress as well as his impending marriage to a sculptress. Besides, how could de la Torre have smothered himself with a plastic bag flawed by a hole?

Reports from the great Southwest compelled artists to suspect everyone. It might be the neighbor, or the unshaven stranger, or the clean-shaven co-worker with the strange eyes, or someone else, it might be anyone. In Scottsdale popular painter of sadistic cowboys and Indians, Rick Osborne, was officially declared a victim of homicide. Police now said they'd been suspicious immediately. That is unlikely. But they'd gotten an anonymous tip that noted the rugged artist not only painted left-handed, he expertly shot his pistols with that hand and would never have placed a gun to his right temple and thereby left a large exit wound on the other side. Furthermore, Osborne had always stated he'd never consider shooting himself until he'd lost his vigor. And at age forty-five, with a young pregnant wife and an even younger mistress, he was still in his prime.

Upon reexamining the cool corpse of Sonia Villarreal, painter of large canvases of depressive females in the nude, the coroner in Santa Fe pronounced he was looking at a murder victim. The lead detective said damn right. No one stabs herself in the heart three times. At least it seemed very unlikely, even accounting for despair, rage, and adrenalin. They'd have to check the literature on that one. But they knew to start looking beyond Villarreal's blood-drenched hand clenching a pallet knife buried in her chest.

In this climate of fear and hysteria, it was inevitable authorities in Sedona conclude that Madge Erickson, one of the finest plein air painters in the region, a master of going right to the source and working fast before the light changed and creating ominous blood red visions of renowned peaks in the area, had been pushed down a steep mountain where she tumbled over numerous sharp rocks before being stopped dead by a boulder near the bottom. There was no physical evidence Erickson had been pushed, but figure it out. She was born and raised in the area, and had hiked and camped there since childhood when she'd begun to paint what her mind saw. She was also an expert outdoorswoman, fit at age forty-two and clear-headed, according to toxicology reports, and never took unreasonable chances. No one had ever seen her set up her easel so close to the edge of a precipice. And had she painted anything? Not a stroke. A blank canvas glared down at the remains of Madge Erickson.

The investigation acquired greater focus when noted New York collector J. Frederick Rutherford called a press conference and announced that prices for works by the murdered artists had quintupled in less than a month. He owned two or more paintings by each and had daily been turning down offers.

"Then, perhaps, that makes you a suspect," stated a writer from *Art Americana Magazine.*

"I'm a billionaire, you buffoon. Find someone who needed market appreciation. And – I say this primarily to authorities – carefully monitor anyone who's marketing works by these artists."

Many people were selling those works, posting hot offers on the internet, carting the paintings to galleries that represented the artists as well as a slew of others now willing to take their work on consignment, contacting the big auctions houses, and/or making quiet deals in closed rooms. Claudette Powell, Madge Erickson's bereaved dealer in Sedona, turned over Madge's list of clients to police before publicly rebuking them for not demanding similar lists from associates of other deceased artists. This task, expedited by the FBI, was complete within days, and computer analysis revealed works by all six artists were owned by only two people – J. Frederick Rutherford and Lyle Perkins.

Less than an hour later numerous squad cars and unmarked cars, an armored vehicle, and three helicopters converged on the big house of Lyle Perkins. Attired only in boxer shorts, Perkins was seated in his living room, reading and annotating a history text for the impending start of school. When the front door collapsed he was instantly surrounded by officers who aimed guns at his head.

"Don't move," an officer warned.

Perkins didn't.

"This guy's a pervert," said another officer, pointing up.

That characterization, at least in the artistic sense, was unfair and uninformed. On his ceiling Perkins had hired carpenters to install a huge tapestry of a pregnant woman, her big belly white and luminescent as she reclined on her side and peered at everyone who looked up.

"The work was done by her husband," Perkins explained.

"Face down on the floor."

Before Perkins could comply two burly officers grabbed him, jerked him into the air and then slammed his nose into the carpet as their comrades charged to other rooms where they found plenty that enraged them. First, every wall was plastered by paintings from floor to vaulted ceiling. Also, the walls in every closet were covered with art, and the floors therein were crowded by paintings, both framed and unframed, that leaned on each other for support. The bathrooms as well were clotted with art. Even Perkins' van was stacked full of paintings, and excess was not all that shocked Perkins' captors. No, the subject matter was even more revolting. Two paintings showed women giving birth to moist and discolored babies. There was a painting of naked Jews being horded into a gas chamber at Auschwitz. There were pictures – by Josephine Bragg of San Francisco – of women brutalized and dead. There were images of beggars, of drunks crawling in the streets, of junkies shooting their veins, of wicked men approaching children, of women and men interacting in startling ways. And, perhaps most disturbing, there were abstract works that to the officers looked like paint had merely been flung and splattered onto the canvases. That in fact had been the means of application. But they didn't understand. Neither did

Perkins. Probably no one understood. No one had understood Jackson Pollock, the master of drip paintings, though many claimed to, and no one understood these stylistic grandchildren of Pollock. There was nothing to understand but plenty to feel.

"We've definitely got our guy," said a man in a suit and a wire in his ear.

Evidence emerged like an avalanche. Perkins had purchased more than five hundred paintings at an average price of about six grand, which represented an outlay of three million dollars, far more than even the shrewdest of teachers could account for. And, unsurprisingly, he had at least fifteen paintings by each of the deceased artists. To achieve this he had acquired scores of credit cards, using a variety of fictitious names as well as the swiped identities of many worried people. All cards, naturally, were maxed out, and he was beyond bankrupt. He in fact was already being investigated for fraud and certain to be convicted. What a piddling charge fraud now seemed.

* * *

A death sentence seemed certain after authorities learned Lyle Perkins' mother had been psychotic, his father an alcoholic who died in the throes of delirium tremens, and his brother a depressive young man who long ago killed himself. Perkins had been spared the worst of the family's inherent pain and seemed cursed only by his very shy nature and an unnaturally pale face red-flagged by an aquiline nose. He'd always compensated by studying very hard in high school and could have attended any university but had instead selected a small Midwestern bible college where he was not overwhelmed and could study all the time without people laughing at him as they had in high school. Though he made no close friends, rarely dated, and didn't lose his virginity, Perkins viewed his undergraduate days as the launching point of his life. He got a history degree and became a high school teacher.

Perkins' social conscience, heightened by reading books by flamboyant black revolutionaries Eldridge Cleaver and George Jackson, had so confused him about his real needs that he'd decided to begin his career at an inner city school in Chicago, and was of course derided or ignored by the students and his contract wasn't renewed. He wouldn't have returned anyway.

He'd moved back to a small town in the Midwest and gotten a job at a Christian school where rules were very strict. Perkins was an effective albeit uninspiring teacher in this environment, and he'd lived frugally for almost twenty years, trading up from small house to medium to damn big, and in all these residences he'd kept an ever-growing collection of framed prints or computer-painted reproductions of works by Raphael, Michelangelo, Rubens, and Velasquez and many other classical masters.

Perkins had also been able to establish two long-term romances, one lasting more than six months and the other almost three years. Both women were shy and plain and thankful to enjoy intense sex with Perkins but were quite put off by his insistence on leaving right after satiation – which usually required him to climax at least three times – or, if they were at his place, his telling them it was time to go. Perkins offered each a chance to move into his big place if she would accept a bedroom on the other side of the house. This not entirely unreasonable offer was in each case rejected not so much because of the proposed sleeping arrangement, which was better than either woman had immediate prospect of bettering, but due to Perkins' obsession with art.

At the start, Perkins' commitment hadn't been alarming. He merely stated that some open spaces on his walls at eye level would be occupied by masterpieces. In his small town Perkins could not obtain much of what he needed, and since he refused to make such critical selections based on magazine photos or images on the internet, he began to fly to big cities to hunt for prints, and during these sojourns eventually discovered the excitement of entering galleries to gaze at real paintings. Then he'd proudly tell numerous art dealers about his collection but they generally sneered and only one expert spoke empathetically. That seminal discussion came at a constellation of galleries in Santa Monica, where a handsome blonde woman invited him into her office.

"Mr..."

"Perkins."

"Mr. Perkins, when you factor in framing and glass, and especially those ghastly computer concoctions, you're spending a lot of money.

Aren't you?"

"Yes, but not like the prices in these galleries."

"You need to learn to shop for a painting just as you would a house. Do you own a house?"

"Yes."

"There you are. You must remember, Mr. Perkins, that an original work of art has intrinsic value that grows forever. And the financial value is often quite significant as well. What you have now, frankly, is worthless."

Perkins had agreed. His works were dead as the people who'd painted them, and not remotely as vibrant as the live works around him in this gallery. What had he been thinking? He'd been tunneled into a bourgeois, Midwest way of thinking that precluded creativity and his building a great art collection.

"I love this artist's work," he said.

"Four years ago, you could have gotten one of his major works for two thousand dollars. These pieces here, which are even better, only cost five thousand. That's more than twenty percent annual appreciation, Mr. Perkins. And we certainly expect that to continue."

"I'll take the one on the left."

"Your study of the masters has given you a discerning eye, Mr. Perkins."

He had chosen a large vertical painting of a woman. You could tell she was a woman though she was partially abstract and reclining into space and comprised of swirls and loose brushstrokes that suggested eternal movement and sexual availability. After tax, and an additional four hundred dollars to ship the painting, Perkins was delighted to ring up well under six grand on his credit card. That was nothing. At last he had real beauty.

* * *

The notoriety of Lyle Perkins attracted many legal suitors, and he was able to hire renowned defense attorney Jimmy Jefferson, who had helped several likely-guilty celebrities walk away from brutal crimes. Jefferson was delighted to take this case for a dollar a week. And he promptly launched his defense through the media, asserting in general terms that Perkins was a sincere and gentle educator and aesthete who had never harmed anyone, not even verbally. Meanwhile, Jefferson's investigative team – funded by eight-figure advances for book and movie deals technically about his involvement in other cases – was studying, interviewing, cajoling, snooping on, and bribing an astonishing array of people, from Perkins' childhood teachers to neighbors past and present to intimates and associates of the decedents. After five weeks, the tuxedo-clad Jefferson held a press conference in his Beverly Hills mansion and proclaimed, "I call on the district attorneys in all six jurisdictions to throw these cases out. They are without merit and at best a smokescreen to hide bungled investigations. It is likely, however, that the people responsible for these investigators couldn't possibly be so incompetent. They therefore are intentionally and criminally framing my client. And that, after the exoneration of Mr. Perkins, will result in our filing civil suits of unprecedented magnitude. Release my client at once, or else."

Authorities had not complied by the first of the scheduled preliminary hearings, in Los Angeles, where Perkins, paler than ever, meekly stated he was not guilty, which everyone had assumed would end the day's proceeding. As they prepared to leave, Jimmy Jefferson jumped out of his chair, thrusting both hands high in the air, the ultimate defender, and shouted, "Your Honor, let us rid ourselves of this farce. Let us cleanse this day with truth that will liberate us all."

"You have something to add, Mr. Jefferson?"

Glancing with bewilderment into the camera and at the courtroom audience, Jefferson said, "Yes, Your Honor, I do have something. Right here in my hand. Look. It's the quite thorough toxicology report by the good authorities here in this municipality, my hometown. Let us take a look. Evidently, the district attorney and police have yet to see it. Or they've chosen to ignore it. Why? So they can frame Mr. Perkins?"

"Objection, Your Honor, objection," shouted the assistant district attorney, standing aerobically fit in her tight pants suit.

"Sustained."

"Fine, Your Honor, I will simply present the facts. On the night of his death, Adelberto Vargas was drunker than hell. How drunk was that? Try a blood alcohol level of .32, four times the legal limit to operate a motor vehicle in California. Only one person could have poured that much alcohol into the stomach of Adelberto Vargas, and that is the decedent himself. Tragically, he had a history of alcoholism dating from his mid-teens, a fact abundantly documented by his relatives, all of whom he was estranged from. Furthermore, Adelberto Vargas was a depressive man. Three times he was confined to psychiatric hospitals for stays ranging from thirty days to six months. He'd threatened suicide on more occasions than anyone could remember. Yes, he had a big bump on his head. That's what happens when you stagger head first into the door frame of your car. Blood and hair were clearly compressed there. And I do not believe authorities were unaware of that."

"Objection."

"Overruled."

"A few of Mr. Vargas' fingerprints have just been detected on the garden hose that ran from the exhaust pipe to the driver's window. His final conscious act was to open the door and place the hose inside, and a divine act of mercy permitted him to be rendered unconscious as he fell bruised head first into his vehicle where he expired.

Your Honor, in the name of a righteous God, I beg you to throw this case out."

"I must reexamine the facts, Mr. Jefferson."

Two days later charges were dropped and Perkins was flown to San Francisco where the case against him was formidable. He'd used one of his credit cards to rent a Union Square hotel room the night Josephine Bragg died. Naturally, he'd also used another card to check into an East LA dive the night before. Jimmy Jefferson wasn't concerned about Perkins' itinerary. Hundreds of millions of people traveled, though no more than a few would have been in all six locations on the very days the artists perished. Perhaps Perkins was the only one. What did that prove? Nothing.

At the preliminary hearing in San Francisco, after Perkins said not guilty, Jimmy Jefferson said, "I would like to call Heidi O'Reilly to the stand."

Ms. O'Reilly, who had been weeping softly in a seat in back of the courtroom, waved him away and wept harder.

"Mr. Jefferson," said the judge, "this is not an appropriate time to question Ms. Bragg's sister."

"Shall we wait until my client has been burned at the stake?"

"Another insult like that, Mr. Jefferson, and I'll hold you in contempt of court."

"I apologize for my emotionality, Your Honor, but I have quite compelling evidence."

"What is it?"

"Heidi O'Reilly is not the sister of Josephine Bragg. Starting at age fourteen, Ms. O'Reilly lived as a foster child in the Bragg household. During that period the two girls became involved, romantically involved, Your Honor."

"That's a lie," O'Reilly stood and shouted.

"Is it, Ms. O'Reilly? Your Honor, I have two witnesses, both in the courtroom today, who had love affairs with Josephine Bragg, and each was threatened with bodily harm by Heidi O'Reilly. This is not mere hearsay. I have, right here on this table, the police reports filed by these women."

"They're lying bitches and weren't good enough for Josie," O'Reilly screamed.

"Calm yourself, Ms. O'Reilly, or I'll have you removed from this courtroom."

"Josie was too trusting and couldn't judge people. She needed me to protect her."

"Then why did you threaten her too?" said Jefferson. "Because she wanted you out of her life. And that's why she also filed several police reports against you. I have three of them right here and can of course get the rest."

Twelve hours later, down at the police station, Heidi O'Reilly confessed.

At his press conference the following afternoon, Jimmy Jefferson said, "I urge authorities in the remaining four jurisdictions to drop all charges against my client. All murder charges, that is. He is indisputably guilty of gross misuse of credit and must pay his bills at once, which he simply cannot do when unjustly confined to jail."

The district attorneys in New York City, Scottsdale, Santa Fe, and Sedona told Jefferson, and more importantly their constituents, that Lyle Perkins had committed heinous crimes – albeit fewer than initially believed – and would not go unpunished. Thus, Jimmy Jefferson and Perkins took their show – and that's what it was, appearing at the start of newscasts and on front pages – to the sacred community of Manhattan.

"Isn't it odd, Your Honor," Jefferson said at the preliminary hearing, "that Mr. Perkins' fingerprints are never at the crime scene? Not a single hair from his head is ever left behind. No blood, no DNA, no witnesses, no rational indications of any kind are ever presented. What we instead have is a trail of tragic coincidences that politically sensitive DAs clutch at in pitiful attempts to convince the world they aren't corrupt and incompetent."

"That's a five thousand dollar fine, Mr. Jefferson, and I cringe thinking about how long you'll be in jail after another inflammatory remark."

"I beg your pardon, Your Honor. The burden of injustice is indeed causing me to say things I regret. This case is still another example. There's no evidence at all linking Mr. Perkins to the death of Alfonso de la Torre. And though I am saddened by the passing of such a talented him, I am more than tired, I am devastated, by uninformed remarks that Alfonso de la Torre was such a happy man he could not have wanted to die."

"The coroner has already ruled that Mr. de la Torre couldn't possibly have smothered himself," said the stern deputy district attorney.

"I accept that Mr. de la Torre didn't kill himself. But he certainly tried. And he had good reason. If authorities had checked medical records at La Raza Medical Clinic, they would've seen that two weeks before his death Mr. de la Torre was diagnosed with terminal brain cancer. His death was certain to be agonizing not only for him but those who would have had to care for him. Alfonso de la Torre cared too much about the quality of life, his and that of Veronica Grant, his fiancée, to permit a protracted and ignominious end. So he placed a plastic bag over his head and hoped to die with dignity but, as we know, the bag had a hole in it. For that reason I must ask that Veronica Grant be called to testify."

From her seat in the audience, with alarming calm, she said, "When I ran in and tore the bag away, he was gasping, he was spitting and gagging and he'd turned the most awful blue, and finally he opened his eyes; they begged me for help. And then he was able to say it: 'For God's sake, finish it.' I put a pillow over his face and would do so again."

"That's admirable, Ms. Grant," Jefferson said, "but why were you going to let the state destroy Mr. Perkins' for your act of mercy?"

"I was afraid. I'm so sorry."

Veronica Grant was taken into custody but the district attorney soon announced that he would file only minor charges and seek no jail time.

District attorneys in the wild Southwest again scrutinized their files and suffered deciding what to do. They could easily place Perkins in their communities at the right time, or at least the right day, but weren't sure what else could they really prove.

"Maybe the sons of bitches should hire Jefferson to solve these crimes," said a caller to a radio talk show in Phoenix.

"Perkins has already done that," said the host.

On this spring day Scottsdale was already hotter than most places in summer, and citizens with sunburned faces crowded the courtroom. When Perkins was brought in, shuffling on manacled legs, helpless hands bound at his belly, many Arizonans pointed and whispered. When Jimmy Jefferson strode in, several applauded, some standing to do so, and the judge ordered them to settle down, and to Jefferson he said: "Counselor, you better behave in my courtroom."

"That I assuredly will, Your Honor, for I know we desire the same thing – justice."

"I used to be a defense attorney, Mr. Jefferson."

"Absolutely, and perhaps you'd have succeeded more often had you not been burdened by guilty clients. My task, admittedly, is far easier. Lyle Perkins is demonstrably innocent."

"You'll have to prove that."

"I beg your pardon. It's my understanding the accused must be proved guilty beyond a reasonable doubt."

"Yes, Mr. Jefferson," said the district attorney, "you bet we're going to do that."

"With the judge's help?"

"That's ten grand right there, Mr. Jefferson. Next time, you're going to the pokey."

"I'd like to call Burl Dawkins to the stand," said the district attorney.

A big handsome man, tanned rather than burned, walked through the short, swinging gate and raised his right hand.

"Mr. Dawkins, you were Rick Osborne's best friend, were you not?"

"I sure was, sir. We'd been close since we were kids. He was a few years older and always looked after me, taught me how to ride, how to shoot, how to paint. I've felt about half a man since he's been gone."

"You're helping his family, aren't you?"

"Yes sir. I'm helping them financially and visiting as often as I can. Rick'd always wanted kids and was so sad it appeared he couldn't, then so happy when his wife finally got pregnant."

"When did you last see Mr. Osborne?"

Dawkins put a big brown hand over his face. "I saw Rick a couple hours before he died."

"Where were you?"

"At our studio. He said he had an appointment."

"Did he tell you who the appointment was with?"

"Yes, he said it was with his most enthusiastic collector, Lyle Perkins."

Gasps rocked the room.

"Rick'd been telling me about this guy who'd bought twenty-six of his paintings, and now wanted a special one on commission. It was going to be seven feet high and ten across, a big story about a group of white men slaughtering some Indian women and children. It would've been a masterpiece."

"Where did Mr. Osborne say he was going?"

"About thirty miles north of here to a place right for the painting."

"I think that's all we'll need today, Your Honor," said the district attorney.

"That's just a warm-up, Your Honor," said Jefferson.

"Very well, Mr. Jefferson."

"Mr. Dawkins, you say you're now helping the family of your best friend."

"That's right."

"How much help?"

"Much as they need."

"That evidently includes staying with them every night."

"Not every night. But Molly needs my help and so does the baby."

"Isn't it remarkable Rick Osborne conceived a baby?"

"It's a miracle from God."

"Please take a look at these medical reports, Mr. Dawkins." Jefferson handed him three file folders. Dawkins kept looking at Jefferson. "Don't bother reading them, Mr. Dawkins. You know what they say."

"Objection."

"Sustained."

"All right, Mr. Dawkins, let me put it like this: do you have any idea what they say?"

"No sir."

"Did you and Mr. Osborne discuss personal matters?"

"We talked about everything."

"So you knew that Mr. Osborne had three times been diagnosed as being permanently sterile?"

"I had no idea."

"But you talked about everything."

"Yeah, but that's not something a man like Rick would've accepted. Thank God the doctors were wrong."

"There's no evidence the doctors were wrong, Mr. Dawkins."

"You should see that beautiful baby."

"I have, in pictures. He looks just like you."

"Objection," shouted the district attorney.

"Sustained. Mr. Jefferson, you're an inch from being handcuffed."

"Your Honor, I've already demonstrated, in three medical documents I urge the court to examine, that Rick Osborne could not have fathered any child. But we needn't argue the point. Let's test. I assert that the father of the child will be Burl Dawkins. I have two witnesses waiting outside, former girlfriends of Mr. Dawkins, who're prepared to testify that Dawkins dropped them, while Rick Osborne was still alive, because of his love for Molly Osborne. That love was, and is, reciprocated. Mr. Dawkins and Molly Osborne are living as man and wife. My investigation, which includes audio and video tapes as well as testimony of neighbors and friends, easily proves that."

"That doesn't prove I killed my best friend, you sonuva bitch."

"That remark just cost you five hundred dollars, Mr. Dawkins," said the judge. "There better not be another."

"Is the child yours, Mr. Dawkins?" said Jefferson.

"Okay, yeah, the kid's mine. But I only donated sperm because Rick asked me to."

"To which doctor did you donate the sperm?"

"I don't remember."

"Did you donate the sperm directly to Mrs. Osborne?"

"Objection, Your Honor."

"Answer the question, Mr. Dawkins."

"Yeah. Rick didn't trust doctors."

"Did Mr. Osborne ever threaten you for impregnating his wife?" Jefferson asked.

"Of course not. He wanted me to."

"Do you know Buddy Anderson?"

"Sure, he's a good friend of ours."

"Last night Mr. Anderson told one of my investigators he'd decided to surprise you guys by dropping by your studio. And as he was about to knock, he heard Mr. Osborne say, 'Fuck my wife again, I'm gonna kill you.'"

"Buddy's lyin."

"I ain't lyin," Buddy called from his seat in courtroom.

Within a week Perkins was on his way to Santa Fe, no decision having been made about either him or Burl Dawkins. But the district attorney said there were only two suspects and the case would remain open until solved.

In many of the more than two hundred art galleries in Santa Fe, Perkins was well remembered for his forgettable appearance and compulsive acquisition of paintings. Of the many talented artists whose work is shown in this vibrant art community, Sonia Villarreal was indisputably Perkins' favorite. She had begun her professional career with a series of beautiful but mundane portraits of herself in the nude. She was a stunning woman, graced with flawless dark brown skin and long silken black hair, and entirely too good looking to convey, with depictions of her face and form, what she was thinking. For that she needed fat models, emaciated models, drunken models, models disfigured by bad breaks at birth or worse thereafter. Sonia Villarreal wanted to paint the real world, the worst of it, and she did. Collectors of commercial art had immediately abandoned her work, but that was fine. She didn't want them. She wanted serious collectors who appreciated serious subjects. Lyle Perkins was such a collector, and often visited her studio in Santa Fe. He always purchased at least one painting, and once bought four in one afternoon.

In court the district attorney asked Lucia Hernandez, a fellow artist and close friend of the decedent, "Did Mr. Perkins ever make a pass at Ms. Villarreal?"

"Yes. The time Mr. Perkins bought four paintings, he asked Sonia to have dinner with him."

"What did she say?"

"She said, 'I'll sell the guy my work, but come on.'"

"What else did Ms. Villarreal say about Mr. Perkins?"

"She said it was weird how many paintings Mr. Perkins was buying and she felt uncomfortable around him and wasn't going to let him in her studio anymore."

"Did Mr. Perkins ever try to get more appointments in her studio?"

"Yes, toward the end he was calling her two or three times a week and telling her how great she was, as an artist and a woman."

"What was Ms. Villarreal's response?"

"She said she was going to change her phone number. That's the last time I talked to her."

"Thank you, Ms. Hernandez."

Jimmy Jefferson was shaking his head and smiling as he walked very close to the witness. "Ms. Hernandez, did you ever invite Mr. Perkins to your studio?"

"Of course not."

"Do you know what this is?"

"It looks like a tape."

"That's right, Ms. Hernandez. It's a tape from Mr. Perkins' phone recorder. Do you know what's on the tape?"

"No, I don't."

"Shall I play it?"

She did not reply. The judge said to proceed. The voice on the tape said, "Mr. Perkins, this is Lucia Hernandez. I'm one of the best artists in Santa Fe, and Sonia Villarreal has told me all about you and I'd like to show you my work the next time you're in town. I can give you some major discounts. I'd also love to just visit with you and talk about art. My phone number is…"

"Well, Ms. Hernandez?"

"I never met the guy."

"You mean Mr. Perkins never called?"

"No."

"Did Mr. Perkins ever comment about your work?"

"Not to me."

"But he did comment to your art dealer, who also represented Ms. Villarreal and still represents her estate, didn't he?"

"I don't know."

"Don't worry, Ms. Hernandez. Claudine Moreau has a splendid memory."

Elegantly attired and heavily made up, the mid-fifties Moreau took the stand and smiled at Jefferson.

"Ms. Moreau, did you ever discuss Lucia Hernandez's work with Mr. Perkins?" Jefferson asked.

"Yes, on several occasions."

"What did Mr. Perkins say?"

"He said he thought Lucia's work much inferior to Sonia's, and that Lucia was stealing Sonia's ideas."

"Did you agree?"

"At first I didn't. But Mr. Perkins eventually convinced me. When I told Lucia I was dropping her from my gallery, she became violent."

"She attacked you?"

"Almost. She rushed at me, cursing, and said Sonia and I were thieves who were jealous of her talent."

"Were you jealous?"

"Of what? Of course not. I tried to help her. Her work never sold well, she's a decent artist, but not one with the power and vision of Sonia Villarreal."

"Did Ms. Hernandez say anything else about Ms. Villarreal?"

"She said she was going to Sonia's that instant?"

"When was that?"

"The last day of Sonia's life."

"All right, quiet down," the judge demanded. Spectators stopped buzzing but tension lingered.

"Did you call Ms. Villarreal to warn her?"

"Oh yes. I was terrified what Lucia might do."

"What was Ms. Villarreal's response?"

"She said she'd call the police if Sonia caused any trouble."

After a long recess, Lucia Hernandez was back on the stand.

"Ms. Hernandez," Jimmy Jefferson said, "did you quarrel with Sonia Villarreal?"

"No, I swear, I didn't. I only told her I was going to overwhelm her artistically."

Jefferson stepped close to Lucia Hernandez and said, "It must have bothered you that Ms. Villarreal's work sold so well."

"Yeah, that's natural. There are probably lots of attorneys jealous of you right now. That doesn't mean they're going to kill you."

"But you would've loved to be as successful as Sonia Villarreal."

"I would've been. I mean, I'm still going to be. Several other galleries are interested in my work. And I'm sure their directors are a lot more dependable than Claudine."

"What do you mean?"

"She never paid on time even though my commissions were small. Sonia really had problems."

This messy situation required further investigation, which revealed that Claudine Moreau had often either short-changed Sonia Villarreal on commissions or withheld them altogether, and that Villarreal had written in a recently-discovered diary about her determination to hire a lawyer and adjudicate this matter. Moreau, who had once been so beautiful men inundated her with money and gifts, was still living like a starlet but without the bonuses. Her business, though modestly successful, could not account for her wardrobe and jewelry and worldwide travel. Authorities continued to examine and reexamine the bloody pallet knife but could find nothing that linked it to Perkins or Moreau or Hernandez. Nevertheless, like their counterparts in Scottsdale, Santa Fe authorities vowed to crack this case.

Meanwhile, Perkins and Jefferson went to Sedona.

"Your Honor," said the district attorney, "I'd like to call Sheriff

Horace Wright to the stand."

Wright raised his right hand and took a seat.

"Sheriff, the family of Madge Erickson recently hired private forensic pathologists to perform an extremely thorough examination."

"Objection," said Jefferson. "I didn't know about it. The defense had every right to be present to verify the accuracy of all procedures."

"It's too late now, Mr. Jefferson," said the judge. "I didn't know either. But I promise you'll have access to all the findings."

"What were the findings, Sheriff?" the district attorney asked.

"Madge Erickson had a small piece of a human tongue in her throat."

"Did you preserve this piece of tongue?"

"Yes sir, it's right over there in a jar in that handbag. Would you like a look?"

"Of course."

"Objection," Jefferson said.

"Overruled," said the judge.

Forensic pathologist Roy Costa was called to testify.

He pointed to a tidbit of dark flesh floating in clear liquid and said, "It's a piece from the tip of a tongue, as if the victim…"

"Objection."

"Sustained."

"Okay, as if the decedent had been…"

"Objection. 'As if' sounds like a fairy tale."

"Stick to what you know," the judge said.

"The piece is quite small, really, and its absence wouldn't impair the man's ability to speak. But the wound would certainly leave scar tissue."

"Mr. Perkins, I'd like to examine your tongue," said the district attorney.

"Objection, Your Honor."

"That's a simple request, Mr. Jefferson," said the judge.

"But Your Honor, even if Mr. Perkins has an injury, he could have sustained it in a variety of ways."

"Then I guess he'll be anxious for DNA to clarify matters," said the judge.

Paint it Blue

Sources

The short stories "In the Blue House" and "The Collector" are from the collection *The Bold Investor*

Homecoming, The Art and Life of William H. Johnson by Richard J. Powell.

Life with Picasso by Francoise Gilot and Carlton Lake.

The Night Tulsa Burned, a documentary film, informs the story "Tulsa Riots."

Room with Curtains is based on *The Dead are here*, a painting on four walls of fourteen-foot tulle curtains by Izhar Patkin.

"Changes in Nude" is based on *Choices*, a painting by Vera Ximinez.

George Thomas Clark

About the Author

George Thomas Clark is the author of *Hitler Here,* an internationally-acclaimed biographical novel, *The Bold Investor, King Donald, In Other Hands, Paint it Blue, Death in the Ring, Obama on Edge,* and *Echoes from Saddam Hussein.*

Clark also follows the news and sports, exercises daily (albeit delicately), collects contemporary art, enjoys independent movies, and travels to places (most recently Madrid, Mexico City, Quito, Guanajuato, and Aguascalientes) where he can socialize in Spanish.

The author's website is GeorgeThomasClark.com

CPSIA information can be obtained
at www.ICGtesting.com
Printed in the USA
LVOW10s1726151217
559880LV00005B/1057/P